BOOK FOUR OF THE SHADOW ORDER

MICHAEL ROBERTSON

Email: subscribers@michaelrobertson.co.uk

Edited by:

Terri King - http://terri-king.wix.com/editing
And
Pauline Nolet - http://www.paulinenolet.com

Cover Design by Dusty Crosley

Michael Robertson
© 2017 Michael Robertson

Eradication - Book four of The Shadow Order is a work of fiction. The characters, incidents, situations, and all dialogue are entirely a product of the author's imagination, or are used fictitiously and are not in any way representative of real people, places or things.

Any resemblance to persons living or dead is entirely coincidental.

All rights reserved

No part of this publication may be reproduced, stored in a retrieval system or transmitted in any form or by any means electronic, mechanical, photocopying, recording or otherwise, without the prior written permission of the author except in the case of brief quotations embodied in critical articles and reviews.

MAILING LIST

Would you like to be notified of my new releases and special offers? Join my mailing list for all of my updates at www.michaelrobertson.co.uk

CHAPTER 1

Seb looked up into the glowing yellow eyes of the huge mech on the other side of the arena. The mech stared right back at him, leaning forwards, looming over him. His hands were cold, but when he balled them into fists, they felt stronger than they ever had, like he could punch through rock … through metal.

Twice Seb's height, if not more, the gigantic steel brute charged at him, the floor shaking beneath its heavy steps. It dipped its head as it ran and clenched its large fists as if in mockery of the puny human form it faced. A massive metal humanoid, each of its balled hands were the size of boulders.

Despite Seb's slow-motion perspective of the fight, the huge beast closed the space between them in a flash. What had been an expanse of clinical-white floor was reduced to just a few metres in a blink. Thankfully, he didn't have to see it move in real time.

Seb scanned the beast's large body, but he couldn't see a weak spot on the chrome monstrosity. When it pulled its right arm back, he did all he could at that moment and ducked its wild swing. Not that avoiding a fight would keep him alive for long; he had to take the thing down somehow.

The mech's momentum carried it past Seb. The vibration of its footsteps ran an earthquake through the floor, blurring his vision. It made it impossible to see the pneumatic pole that punched from its waist. As thick as Seb's torso, it jabbed into his side, driving the wind from his body and sending him flying across the arena as if he weighed nothing.

Seb's entire skeleton shook with the vibration of hitting the wall and nausea clamped tight in his guts. The metallic taste of his own blood flooded his mouth.

A second or two passed where Seb fought to stay conscious. Were it not for the heavy steps descending on him again, he might have let himself black out completely.

Standing up on wobbly legs, Seb pulled a deep breath into his lungs. After spitting a mouthful of red on the white floor, he fought to get his breath back as the mech closed on him once again.

The brute lifted both of its large fists this time, its glowing eyes fixed on Seb as it charged forward. Its silence as it ran unnerved Seb more than anything. Sure, the effect of its actions made sounds, but whenever he'd had an opponent, he could hear their struggle in their grunts and snarls. He could measure their fatigue. The mech fought with a cold and clinical detachment. The only tiredness this opponent would feel would come when its batteries drained. Designed to bring about his utter destruction, and clearly more than capable of the task, it brought its fists crashing down at him.

Seb rolled to the side and jumped to his feet again. The boom of the mech's blow shook the arena, and he struggled to remain upright. Cracks splintered away from where the mech hit the floor and streaked through the white expanse as if the hard concrete was made of glass. The blow would have turned him to mist had he been caught beneath it.

A glance up at the window to the spectator area and Seb saw Moses smiling down on the fight. Acid burned in his guts to watch the smug grin on his shark face.

Deceptively fast for its size, the mech spun on Seb again. Its plain chrome body no doubt hid more surprises like the battering ram in its waist. It picked up speed as it charged forward.

Seb pulled in a deep breath of the bleach-scented air and waited as the creature closed in on him.

At the last moment, he rolled to the side again to avoid another hard attack. The entire arena shook again, the windows to the spectator area buzzing from the second pounding against the floor. It left a similar crater to the first one.

Now the gargantuan had its back to Seb, he darted forward and landed two quick punches to the beast's kidney area. His blows felt cold and hard, and they left two large dents on the monster's chrome body. If he punched any harder, it felt like he could get through the mech's outer shell. Although, despite his power, it seemed to only do cosmetic damage to the large figure. It hadn't slowed it down one jot.

The mech turned around and ran at him again. A circular saw popped from its waist. The mech wore it like a spinning tutu. The galaxy's most dangerous Swiss Army knife, Seb gulped to look at its latest weapon.

The saw blade rotated so fast it turned into a blur, even in slow motion. The high-pitched whine of it bounced around the enclosed space like a dentist's drill; the scream of it turned his knees weak.

With no other way to avoid it, Seb slid through the mech's legs, punching the panel covering its right calf on his way past.

The panel flew off with his heavy blow and clanged against the hard floor. It exposed wires and pneumatics. Like the strikes to its kidneys, it did nothing to slow the thing down.

Another charge at Seb, the mech dropped to its knees and slid at him this time. It blocked off his route between its legs, the circular blade coming forward with the large chrome beast.

A glance at the observation window. This time, Seb made eye contact with Moses. His black eyes. His shark-like head. His huge toothy grin.

Seb kicked off the wall behind him and dived over the top of the mech, just about clearing it as it crashed into the barrier he'd used to vault off. Its circular saw bit into the steel wall. It would have turned him into fleshy confetti had he gotten in the way of it.

As Seb recovered his breath, he watched the mech detach from the steel barrier, stand up, and spin around to face him yet again. It might have been battered, but it still showed no sign of fatigue.

The mech's front then lit up like the sun. What had seemed like a chrome panel now revealed a bright bank of LED lights inside it. They would have dazzled him anyway, but in the stark-white space, they damn near burned his retinas out.

Seb covered his eyes and had to judge the mech's next approach based on the vibrations shaking through the floor at him. He waited, adrenaline telling him to make a run for it, but he held his space. He couldn't go too soon.

When he couldn't wait any longer, the vibrations in the floor close to robbing the strength from his legs, Seb darted to one side.

Another loud crash as the mech connected with the wall

behind where Seb had been. The wind from the spinning blade ran just past his torso.

The mech faced the wall, its back to Seb again. Its lights still turned the space bright, but it allowed him to see better because he wasn't directly in its glare. He took his opportunity and rushed at it.

Just one chance to get it right, Seb punched the top of the circular saw blade as it spun. He hit it so hard, it curled down and bit into the monster's thighs, still spinning as fast as before.

It took just seconds for the blade to eat into the metal body of the mech. The already high-pitched dentist drill whine lifted another octave higher, and the operator screamed before shutting the thing down.

The large metal shell fell onto its back. A toppled tree, it hit the white floor with a loud thud.

Still gripped with fury, Seb rushed over to the mech and punched it repeatedly, denting its shiny chrome body with each blow. He pulled panels away from it every time one of them came loose, which revealed a network of wires and electronics inside.

Once he'd ripped the cold faceplate away, Seb raised his fist but stopped just before he drove a blow into the operator's nose. "You're just a kid."

"I'm twenty-one," the girl said, a scowl of indignation on her tanned features.

"Well, excuse me, Twenty-one. With all that life experience, you must be a hardened warrior by now. What the *hell* are you doing in this suit?"

"Training."

Seb still had his fist clenched and raised above her. To look into her dark and scared eyes helped dilute his fury and he lowered his threat, relaxing, but continuing to sit on top of her. "Well, you need to do better."

"I had you on the ropes."

Seb couldn't help but smile. "You've got spirit, Twenty-one." He then got off the broad, chrome chest of the huge mech and walked towards the arena's exit.

Were it not for the *whoosh* of the jets, Seb would have missed it. It came so quickly his gift didn't kick in. Fortunately, he instinctively threw himself on the floor.

The large rocket crashed into the white wall in front of Seb, igniting into a huge ball of flames and leaving a black scorch mark as big as a doorway on it.

"What the hell?" Seb screamed when he got up. His world slipped into slow motion as he ran back at the downed mech. The thick smoke made his eyes water.

He watched the girl shake her head as he got close. She mouthed something he couldn't understand, the words coming out in long and drawn-out syllables as he watched them through his slowed-down perspective.

Over her again, Seb raised his fist at the girl once more, and everything returned to a normal speed. "What was that about? Are you trying to kill me? What's wrong with you?"

It took a second for her to speak through what looked like a panic attack, tears forming in her dark eyes. After a look up at the observation window, she said, "Please, Moses told me to keep attacking you. I'm only supposed to stop when *he* tells me to. He said that whatever happened, I *had* to keep fighting."

Heavy breaths rocked through Seb and he turned to look up at the leader of the Shadow Order. His voice echoed around the minimalist space. "You gonna say stop now? Or do I have to kill her to prove you don't care about anyone?"

The same cold, detached, onyx stare fixed on him. The

large brute watched on from the comfort of the observation room. The silence hung between them before Moses finally leaned down towards a microphone and pressed a button.

The sound of Moses' heavy breaths swirled around the large space. It shot out at them from a hundred invisible speakers. The leader of the Shadow Order continued to stare at Seb. He then grinned wider than ever and said, "Stop."

CHAPTER 2

The long, white corridor stood as sparse as the arenas it overlooked. Like the arenas, it stank of bleach. Clinical, it reminded Seb of a hospital rather than a training complex.

Large windows afforded views down into the fighting gyms like the one Seb had just battled in. As he walked beside Moses, he glanced down into one of the occupied spaces. Two mechs—each as large as the one Seb had just fought—flew around the place, sending flames and laser fire at one another.

To think of his fight only minutes ago made Seb ball his cold fists. How far did Moses want the girl to go? Would he have let her kill him?

The click of their heels called along the deserted corridor. A sharp reminder they were alone at that moment. Seb looked up at Moses, clenched his jaw, and felt the tension in his already tight fists run up into his shoulders. Despite Moses standing over ten feet tall—a good four feet taller than Seb—he'd still knock the creature out. At least twice his weight, a face full of razor-sharp teeth and a thick hide made no difference, Moses would drop like a felled tree if hit in the correct place.

When Moses looked back, he nodded down at Seb's fists and raised an eyebrow. In a calm, rumbling baritone, he said, "What you planning, boy?"

Call him *boy* again and he'd find out. A deep breath and Seb turned away, looking down into one of the arenas as they passed it. He saw just one being with two blasters shooting small flying droids from the sky as they appeared from the walls at random intervals. Gurt would have smashed that simulation. The slight ache of a lump lifted in Seb's throat to think about his friend.

"You understand we needed to test those hands, right?" Moses said. "You're looking at me like a petulant teenager. Like you don't understand why I told Reyes to give you everything she had. How else could we test those things out? We had to do a lot of surgery on them after your personal war on Solsans. Better to find they don't work now than in the middle of a battle."

"And what better way to test it. I mean, what's my life worth anyway?"

"I knew she wouldn't be able to kill you."

Seb looked down at his hands while he opened and closed them. No sign of bruising from the recent fight, and no signs of damage from the war on Solsans. "What did you do to them?"

"How do they feel?" Moses said.

After he'd opened and closed them a couple more times, Seb said, "Cold."

"They're metal."

"They're *what*?!"

A look at Seb through his detached onyx glare and Moses said, "When you came back from Solsans, they were like two bags of stones. Your bones were so destroyed, we had no way of repairing them. And if we did, they would have been as fragile as porcelain. So we rebuilt them. We remade the bones with steel."

Again, Seb stared at his hands, testing their movement by flexing his fingers while he listened to Moses.

"We also fused your skin with a synthetic material to prevent it from tearing. We removed all the feeling from the back of your hands. You should be able to punch through walls now with those things. You won't feel any pain, and your skin won't show a single blemish. We're turning you into a superhero, Seb."

Seb stopped walking and glared at Moses. "Superheroes fight for *good*, Moses. Not credits."

When Moses didn't respond, Seb touched the tips of his thumbs against the tips of his fingers. He worked up and down his hands several times to be sure. "But you've kept the feeling in my fingers and palms."

"Of course."

"My hands feel much heavier. I assumed it was because my arms were sore rather than the weight of my fists."

"Your muscles will learn to accommodate them. Soon, it won't feel any different."

The conversation dropped off and Seb continued to focus on his cold fists. He looked down into the next arena to see two beings fighting hand to hand. They were mismatched in size. It would have been like Sparks fighting Moses. But from what Seb could see, and the flurry of punches he noticed in the brief moment he passed the arena, the smaller one had the beating of the larger one. Never judge a book and all that.

"I thought you were going to kill Reyes," Moses said.

"You didn't want that?"

"What kind of monster do you think I am?"

Seb chose not to respond.

While staring ahead with a deep scowl, Moses sighed. "Anyway, it was good practice for Reyes too. She needs to learn how to handle mechs. We're training her up so she might be of some use to us. Although I'm not confident she will be. I only took her on because I knew her dad."

"Knew?"

"He's dead now. He was a great Marine. He asked me to take her in and look after her. It was his dying wish."

"And that's how you look after people? You put their lives in danger in fighting arenas? You keep a promise to a dying friend by throwing his daughter into the flames."

Moses stopped dead, looked at Seb, and cocked his eyebrow. "Firstly, you think too highly of yourself. You're *not* the flames. And secondly, what would you have me do? Follow your lead by taking her into an unnecessary war and maybe get her killed in the process?"

Seb threw his hands up at Moses. "Unnecessary? What are you talking about, you moron? Did you see what the Countess did to the people of Solsans?"

Moses bared his teeth. The wide stretch of glistening white would take Seb's head clean off with one bite. The low growl in his voice damn near shook the walls. "Careful, Seb. I still run this place."

But Seb didn't care. Screw him. "You wouldn't be calling that war unnecessary if the slum dwellers in Caloon paid us."

For the next few seconds, Moses stared at Seb. He didn't deny the accusation. Finally, he said, "I'm still not happy about what you did. You went against my orders."

"And I'd do it again."

"If you do, don't expect the same leniency from me."

At that moment, two Shadow Order soldiers walked up the corridor. The snap of their heels did enough to pull Moses and Seb's attention away from one another as they looked at them. The soldiers seemed to pick up on the tense atmosphere. They both dropped their eyes to the ground and scuttled past the pair.

They hadn't gone far past them when Seb said, "I don't care about your threats. I'd do it again in a heartbeat."

A raised eyebrow and Moses shrugged. "You'd kill Gurt again?"

Seb's heart raced and his lungs tightened as if his grief flooded into them. His voice wavered. "I didn't ask him to come back for me."

"No, Seb, you didn't. But he did. Gurt had honour. If you understood that, you would have seen you didn't give him a choice. He *had* to come back for you. It's what any soldier worth their salt would have done. But I wouldn't expect *you* to understand that."

"Like you know about honour. You're a whore to the highest bidder."

"Thin ice, Seb. Very thin ice."

Although Seb opened his mouth to reply, Moses cut him off. "We have a mission planned for you."

The aches from Solsans suddenly returned. They pulled on Seb's body, reminding him of his fatigue. "So soon?"

"It wouldn't have been soon if you'd returned when you were supposed to. We'd planned to give you a couple of days R and R."

Moses moved off again and Seb fell into stride with him. "How many more missions do I need to do for the Shadow Order?"

A deep booming laugh, it ran both ways along the corridor before Moses stopped again. "You've only done one job. Besides, what would you be doing otherwise? Fighting for small amounts of money in pits in the middle of nowhere? Don't pretend you have something better to do."

Seb balled his fists again and glared at the huge shark-like creature. "Finding something better than this isn't hard. Don't flatter yourself."

After a shake of his head, Moses said, "Go and find the others and meet me in thirty minutes in the briefing room." Before Seb could say anything else, the brute spun on his heel and walked away.

Still with an argument in him, Seb fought against his urge to run after Moses. Who did he think he was bossing him around like that? Although, in reality, what could he do at that moment? Refuse and he'd be back in prison.

Streaks of pain ran up either side of Seb's face from where he'd clenched his jaw for the entire conversation. A shake of his head and he walked towards the canteen. Since he'd come back to the Shadow Order's complex, he'd avoided the place. It wouldn't be the same in there without Gurt giving him a hard time.

CHAPTER 3

The second Seb walked into the canteen, he found SA, Sparks, and Bruke. He sat with them and ate a well-earned meal of snork pie and walabi root chips before he led them to the briefing room as Moses had requested.

Seb entered the cold room first and baulked at Moses' steely glare.

A flash of his sharp teeth, Moses spoke in a deep growl. "You're late."

Taken over with faux surprise, Seb suppressed his smile as he pressed a hand against his chest and said, "I'm sorry." A glance at the clock on the wall and he smiled again. "I thought you said to see you in forty-five minutes."

Silence for a moment as Moses tilted his head to one side. Hard to read the black stare he levelled on him, Seb waited until the shark eventually spoke. "I said *thirty*."

While holding his glare, Seb flashed another facetious smile at the beast. "Terribly sorry, old chap. My mistake. It must be all those ferocious teeth in your mouth. They make it hard to hear you sometimes." He lowered his voice and spoke as if sharing a secret with the Shadow Order's leader. "But they are *ever* so scary, so it makes the sacrifice worthwhile, eh?"

Near silence fell over the small room as Seb led the others down to the seats at the front. Although he felt Moses continue to stare at him, he didn't give him the satisfaction of looking back.

When they'd settled, Seb watched Moses open his mouth. He cut him off just before he could speak. "It's a bit cold in here. Can someone turn the air conditioning down?"

A deep breath swelled Moses' already broad chest and he let the silence hang again. He then pulled a three-dimensional image from a computer and projected it in front of the team. A large red globe spinning on its axis appeared, showing them its flame red surface.

"Looks nice," Seb said as he screwed his face up at the seemingly hostile planet. "We've got our first Shadow Order holiday there, have we? Do they have a booze cruise?"

SA and Sparks remained impassive to Seb's goading of their leader. Bruke, on the other hand, tensed in his seat, his back straightening a little more than before. Although Seb felt his scaled friend look at him, he ignored his attention.

"This is the planet Carstic," Moses said. He sped up the spinning image with a bat of one of his large hands. "It's a hostile environment where you have to wear radiation suits outside. Any time in their atmosphere without one and you'll be covered in tumours within ten minutes then die soon after."

"Sounds like Blackpool Pleasure Beach," Seb said.

Everyone turned to look at him, the reference to an old seaside resort on Earth clearly lost on them. Seb only knew it by reputation. They say the apocalypse hit there long before it swept across the rest of the planet.

"What matters," Moses said with a hard exhale that slumped his broad shoulders, "is it's a rough place to visit."

The clap of Seb's hands snapped through the room when he brought them together and squealed. "How wonderful." Before Moses could speak, he added, "And you know what? I don't think I've ever brought cancer back from a holiday before."

Even Bruke ignored him this time.

"There's a mining colony on this planet," Moses said. "Its walls are lined with lead, which keeps the radiation out."

Moses raised his hand at the image of Carstic, his fingers pinched together. He then opened his pinch wide, zooming in on the planet. It showed a large structure with a huge shutter door at the front. It looked like some sort of hangar in the middle of the hostile terrain. It jutted from the ground and seemed large enough for ships to land inside.

"So why are we going there?" Seb said.

Moses stared at Seb as if trying to work out if he was winding him up. After a few seconds, he sighed. "A parasite has got into the colony. It's wiped everyone out."

"What were they mining for?" Sparks asked.

"A natural gas called *ruthane*. It's such a powerful fuel you can run ships on it at a tenth of their normal running cost."

Already magnified through her glasses, Sparks' purple eyes spread even wider. "So it's highly explosive?"

"Yep."

Seb watched his small friend turn pale before he asked Moses, "So no blasters?"

Another spreading of his pinched fingers allowed Moses to take them farther into the colony. They went through the hangar past several ships and tanks parked up inside, and dived down into an underground section. Among other things, it had a toilet block, a shower block, and rooms with beds in.

"There are three areas to the colony," Moses said. "They should all be sealed off from one another. The first section is where the people slept. There are gas readings on the screens before you enter each area, so you'll know when you get there, but we believe each section is still sealed. You should be able to use your weapons in the first two areas without any problems."

"What's in the second section?" Sparks said.

A wave of his hand and Moses took them deeper into the complex. "This is the recreational area. They have a sports hall, games room, and canteen down there. The third section is where they pull the ruthane from the ground. That's a blaster-free zone. Let a shot off down there and you'll turn the entire planet into a flaming ball."

Although Sparks didn't say anything, she stiffened in her seat next to Seb.

"So we're going there to …?" Seb said.

"Eradicate the parasites and clean the place up. We need to get a new community down there capturing the ruthane. The people who own this planet will pay a lot of money to get their supply back."

"Ruthane's that valuable, is it?" Seb said.

Moses offered a monotone reply. "Obviously. You think we'd be going to this shit hole if it wasn't?"

Another chill snapped through Seb. "Is there seriously nothing you can do with the AC?"

Silence.

"Okay," Seb said. "So that's why we're going in rather than just turning the entire planet to dust?"

"Obviously," Moses said again. "Any more inane questions?"

"Actually," Seb said, "I do have one more." A look at his team and then back to Moses and Seb leaned towards the large shark-like creature. "Does this planet have anything to do with the Camorons?"

Silence met Seb's question for a few seconds before Moses finally said, "Yes."

"What are we, their employees or something? Are you their little pet?"

Tension snapped through the room, and even SA squirmed in her seat this time.

"I ain't no one's pet," Moses said. "You'd do well to remember that. The Camorons pay well. We work for credits. It isn't any more complicated than that. Now, are you done?"

Before Seb could say anything else, Moses produced a glass case about the size of a shoebox. It had a grub inside about six centimetres long. It looked dead.

"What's that?" Seb said as he reached forward and tapped on the glass.

The grub exploded to life, launching itself at Seb as if it had been loaded up with ruthane. It hit the glass with a *tock* and fell back to the bottom of the box, stunned. A few seconds later, it recovered and went at him again as if getting to Seb were its sole purpose. Seb pulled back from the violent thing. The sound of its hard, little body tapped again and again against its glass prison.

"We don't know where these things have come from, but they've taken over Carstic." Moses put the glass box down, screwed up the image of the planet he'd left floating in mid-air, and brought up some recorded footage on the screen at the front of the room.

Seb squirmed as he looked at what appeared to be a CCTV recording. It wouldn't be a pleasurable viewing experience, that much seemed obvious. It made it even worse that the footage focused on what looked to be a dad and his daughter. Dryness spread through Seb's mouth, and although he wanted to look away, he didn't.

"We've slowed this down so you can see what you're looking at." Moses drew a line with his thick finger, tracing one of the worm creatures as it flew across the screen at the dad in the shot. The dad had his back turned to the thing. "This is one of the worms. One of the first ones we've captured footage of."

The worm hit the man's back.

"They move as quickly as a fired bullet," Moses said, "and cut through flesh like one."

The man on the screen arched his spine from the impact of the creature and screamed. The little girl next to him couldn't have been any more than about six years old. She screamed too.

"But it hasn't killed him?" Seb said.

"No," Moses replied. "I'm sure he wished it had though."

A twist of nausea tightened in Seb's stomach.

The man on the screen roared. Then, a few seconds later —and even through the grainy footage—Seb saw his red eyes when he turned to face the camera.

A hunched frame and with heavy breaths rocking through him, the man then spun on the little girl. He pounced on her and bit into her throat. The small girl twisted and fitted against his attack, her fight kicking through her spasming limbs. She tried to push him back with her small hands, but then the fight left her and she turned floppy.

The man dropped the little girl and she fell limp on the ground. Her blood ran from his chin.

Seb's breath caught in his throat as he watched the girl lie still. Then another worm flew across the screen and bored into her.

In the blink of an eye, the girl went from seemingly dead to jumping upright. She screamed and hunched over as if looking for someone to attack. A snarl sat on her previously innocent face. Her eyes burned with the same rage as her dad's.

"And that's what we have to fight?" Bruke said, his voice wavering as he watched the footage.

Moses nodded and let out a sombre, "Yep."

The small girl focused on the camera as if she knew they were being filmed. She bared her teeth before she ran straight at the screen.

Seb jumped back in his seat when she leapt impossibly high, grabbed the front of the camera, and yanked it.

The screen turned black as the connection was severed.

Not even Seb had anything to say, and silence fell on the room.

CHAPTER 4

Seb, SA, Sparks, and Bruke all stared at the now blank screen. Were it not for the sound of Moses' heavy breathing through his conical, yet stumpy snout, there would have been complete silence in the room.

The cold bite of the air conditioning added to Seb's discomfort and he nearly asked Moses to turn it down again. Although, he knew the air conditioning served as a distraction for a deeper discomfort within him. No matter how much he squirmed on his chair, he couldn't wriggle away from the image of the little girl with the blood-red eyes. He'd take that sight to the grave. Even when he blinked, her crimson glare flashed through his mind.

When Moses cleared his throat, Seb snapped out of his thoughts with a jump and looked up at the shark-like creature.

"There have only ever been humans on Carstic," Moses said. "The place was uninhabited until the Camorons found ruthane. Humans took the job to mine it."

An ironic laugh and Seb said, "We get all the good jobs, don't we?"

The same cold, onyx glare fixed on Seb. Devoid of any emotion other than rage, Moses stared down at him in his seat. After a few seconds, he said, "My point is that as long as you stay underground in the complex, you'll be perfectly safe from radiation. And if a human can withstand it down there with their precious little immune systems, then you others should be okay too."

Seb looked up at Moses, who flashed a wide grin down at him. For the first time that day, he chose not to react.

"There haven't been any reports of any humans getting ill," Moses added.

"Did you *see* that footage?!" Seb said while pointing at the black screen. "Are you trying to tell me that wasn't ill? I mean, correct me if I'm wrong, but I'd class turning into a zombie as ill. I dunno about you."

"They're not zombies," Moses said. "They've been taken over by parasites." After a pause, he added, "Besides, *zombies*? You're not in a video game."

"You're right." After Seb released a long sigh, he added, "If we were, we'd have more than one life to take down there with us. There ain't no extra credits where we're going."

A few seconds passed where Moses breathed through his nose. A snort rode his heavy breaths as he clearly became more agitated. "What I *mean* is the lead lining will keep you safe from radiation like it has kept the humans down there safe."

The glass case with the grub thing sat on the floor. Seb looked at it as he said, "It won't keep us safe from those creatures though, will it? Now I've seen what they can do, I think I'd rather take my chances with a thousand tumours out in the desert, thanks." Although he watched Moses, he caught Bruke nodding in his peripheral vision.

Moses looked up at the styrofoam ceiling tiles and drew another deep breath before he returned his focus to Seb. "The fact that only humans have ever worked there means you'll know your opponent. Sure, they're infected and seem dangerous, but they're only humans."

"You think our opponents are the *humans* down there?" Seb stood up and Moses tensed, his thick shoulders lifting as if readying himself for a fight.

The attention of the room on him, Seb walked over to the glass box with the grub in it. He tapped the case and the grub exploded to life again. It collided with the inside of its clear prison and the entire container shifted about half a metre forward from the impact. "I'm not sure I agree with you about who our enemy is."

As Seb watched the creature in the box losing the plot, repeatedly crashing into the glass case to get at him, he thought of the red-eyed girl. A look first at Moses and then the others, his teammates all staring at the fitting grub in the box, and Seb returned to his seat.

The cold air conditioning wound through Seb again, and the seat felt more uncomfortable than ever. When he finally looked back at Moses, he found himself in the spotlight of the creature's angry glare. Nothing unusual there. "Are there any survivors?" he said.

A few seconds later, Moses spoke with a slight resignation in his deep voice. "Not that we know of."

Bruke let out one of his anxious whines and snapped tense in his seat.

A look at his scaled friend and Seb saw him sit pole straight. Sparks wrung her hands, and even SA frowned. When he returned his attention to Moses, he shook his head. "I'm not doing it."

Moses leaned forward, his scowl as fierce as ever, his voice so deep it seemed to shake the flimsy walls of the briefing room. "I'm sorry?"

"Don't be sorry."

"Stop being smart."

Seb pointed at the floor. "Smart is staying here and not going anywhere near that bloody planet. Smart is recognising ruthane is never as important as my life, especially as we're only going so the Camorons can make more money. Send George again, he seems perfectly capable."

Moses opened and closed his large fists, his jaw widening and then easing off as he clenched it. "You know I'm not offering you a choice, right?"

"There's always a choice, Jaws."

Bruke flinched next to Seb.

Moses bared his teeth and rushed forward. "Not when you belong to me there ain't."

The smell of fish forced Seb to turn his face to the side. After a few seconds, he pinched his nose against the reek. "Can you step back a pace, big man?"

To Seb's surprise, Moses did as he asked.

"Thank you. It's still no though. I'll say it again; have you *seen* the footage you've just shown us?"

"Of course."

"Well, it shouldn't be a surprise to you as to why I won't go, then."

"You want to go back to a prison cell?"

The little girl with the red eyes flashed through Seb's mind again. "A prison cell seems like a better place to be than that damn mining community. So, yeah, why not? Lock me up. I'd rather be in a cell than in that place. Especially as the only reason we're going there is because someone's paying us."

"That's the only reason to do anything," Moses said.

"For *you* maybe. I ain't risking my life for a few credits. There's nothing there to rescue other than gas. Ruthane ain't that important to me."

CHAPTER 5

"You sure you want this?" Moses said as they stood outside the prison cell. The large steel door in front of them might have worn its rust like psoriasis, but it still stood strong enough to only be opened when the guards wanted it opened. If Seb stepped inside, someone else would decide when he came out again.

After a pause, Seb shook his head. "Of course I don't, but if it's a choice between a prison cell with three square meals a day, or the carcinogenic Carstic full of zombies, I'll take the prison cell, thanks."

The now familiar low growl—so deep Seb felt it in his chest and it blurred his vision—and Moses turned away from him. Six guards had led Seb to the cell, three of them with long cattle prods. They raised them in Seb's direction again to show him they weren't afraid to use them. In fact, if the wicked glints in their eyes were any indication of how they felt, they'd relish the opportunity.

One of the guards opened the door and the others waved the blue ends of their prods at him. Seb raised his hands in defence. "I know it must make you feel powerful to wave them at me, but don't kid yourselves, I'm choosing to walk into this cell. It has nothing to do with your threats. If I wanted to, I'd drop every one of you and walk away. Know that I'm the one making the decisions here, not you."

Three dark scowls responded to Seb, so he walked into the cell backwards to keep an eye on them. They looked like the kind to prod him in the kidneys if he left an opening.

The second Seb crossed the cell's threshold, he baulked at the smell of sweat and shit. Although he felt the tight press of bodies around him—and was tempted to look at them—he kept his attention on the guards with the prods.

When they closed the door and the lock clicked shut, Seb finally turned around to face the other prisoners.

There were about twenty-five beings in total in the small room. All of them were scarred, dirty, and angry. Each of them stared at Seb like he'd been the one to land them there.

Even amongst the press of bodies, Seb saw the mandulu in the corner. Just one bed in the room, he sat on it like the king of the dump.

The cell looked to be about the same size as the one on the *Black Hole*. A couple of metres wide and maybe three metres long, it had dirty white walls where at least half of the paint had peeled off them. The cell Seb had shared on the *Black Hole* had been with just one mandulu. Even then it had seemed crowded. Other than the bed and metal toilet, the room had no other features.

The tension surrounding Seb made it hard to believe it wouldn't kick off at some point. He inhaled the shitty air and looked at each prisoner in turn, his heart rate slightly elevated in anticipation of the fight. He didn't want to fall out with them, but he wouldn't be pushed around. If the glares on their faces were anything to go by, they looked like they wanted to push him.

In a space in the middle of the room, Seb found himself surrounded on all sides. A look around the small cell showed him he had nowhere else to go. As if operating on a hive mind, the creatures stepped closer to him, cutting off what little personal space he had. Halitosis added to the reek of sweat and shit, the hot breath of several of the creatures pushing against him, turning his skin clammy.

The press of bodies consisted of creatures from all over the galaxy. Seb did his best to ignore them and focused on one corner in the room. If he made his way over to there, he could put his back against the wall and only have to fight what came at him from the front.

However, when Seb stepped towards one of the corners, a large beast blocked his way. A wall of a creature, it had a broad chest, brown, leathery skin, and looked down at him, its hands on its hips.

The beast had bright yellow eyes. They looked feline as it glared confrontation at Seb. A simple shake of its head told Seb his plan wouldn't pan out. It remained rooted to the spot.

When Seb looked for somewhere else to move to, the creatures around him closed in another step. He had nowhere to go. The edges of his world blurred as everything shifted into slow motion. If he needed to fight, he would.

Seb returned his attention to the brown, leathery creature. As the largest thing in the room, it made sense to focus on it. Dominate the strongest of the pack and the others would often yield. He pushed a strong hand against its upper right arm and shoved it to one side. He stared into its cat eyes the entire time, which seemed to catch the brute off guard. It raised its top lip in a snarl, but it went with his encouragement and moved out of his way. The look of shock on its brutish face suggested it surprised even itself.

Seeing several creatures behind it, Seb shoved them all

aside as he moved over to one of the corners, turned around so he faced outwards, and pressed his back against the wall.

Every being in the cell continued to watch him, including the mandulu on the bed.

"This is going to get old very quickly," Seb said to the room.

Many of the creatures bristled at him addressing them.

"What is it that's upset you all?" He smiled. "It's got to be that I'm so much prettier than you lot, right?"

A look over the stinking crowd and Seb laughed. "Although, I'm probably prettier than you lot simply because I've washed today. I suppose it's a low bar."

"It's because you're *human*!"

When the crowd parted, Seb stared at the mandulu in the corner on the bed. "Ah, so you're the leader of this band of degenerates, eh? You've got your throne, I see." A look over the rusty bed frame and soiled mattress and he raised his eyebrows. "Very nice; you must be proud."

Deep scars covered the mandulu's fat face. It scowled, pushing its broken horns up over its top lip. Two angry red tracks ran where its horns had cut into its thick skin again and again. He obviously frowned a lot.

After he'd laughed at the creature's show of aggression, Seb said, "Okay, let me humour your sour mood a little, then, yeah?"

The mandulu didn't reply, its frown deepening.

"I'm human. So, what, that makes me responsible for all the actions of my species? I belong to a greedy, paranoid, self-destructive, warmongering race, so I must be greedy, paranoid, self-destructive, and warmongering myself, right?"

Again, the mandulu said nothing.

"I've met some pretty vile mandulus in my time. Actually, all of them have been horrible." To think of Gurt made Seb smile. If the brute could hear him now. "Even the ones I liked were nasty. So does that mean I should judge you because of my experience?"

Before the mandulu could respond, Seb said, "Actually, don't answer that. I suppose it does and I suppose I already have."

The mandulu getting to his feet stirred up the creatures in the cell. He stepped forward a pace, as did all the others.

Seb took in the crowd again. Some of them, like the brown, leathery beast, stood much taller than he did. Some were only half his height or less. All of them had the scars and bruises to show they'd probably earned their spot in that cell. Not that he had that much faith in the justice system on Aloo. One thing seemed certain; they all looked like they'd fight if they needed to.

Despite his cocksure approach, sweat lifted beneath Seb's collar and his throat dried. He'd take on any one of the creatures on their own ... but all of them at the same time ... Little point in thinking about it. He could hardly back down now.

Although none of the creatures moved any closer than their first step, their reluctance appeared to have little to do with fear. They seemed to be waiting for the nod from the mandulu.

"What's the key to your happiness?" Seb said to the large broken-horned beast. When he didn't respond, he added, "I can see the joy you're clearly living with and I'd like some for myself. Come on, big man, don't hold out on me."

The mandulu frowned harder still, almost hiding his features in a mass of wrinkles. Seb looked at some of the other creatures in the space—the one with the cat eyes, another three mandulus, a creature that looked like Bruke but hairy—and he saw they all leaned towards him. They all wore the same furious scowl, and they all looked like they were desperate to take a swing at him. They just needed the word from their leader.

"You need to learn when to shut up," the mandulu finally said.

A frantic nod and Seb laughed. "You've got me. That's exactly what I need to learn to do. I'm a nightmare. I've been like it since childhood. Whenever I get backed into a corner, I start mouthing off." His own pulse ran so hard through him it damn near deafened him, but he kept going. "But you know what? I *always* win, so it's hard to learn the lessons. I'll tell you what"—he stepped towards the beast with his arms wide—"how about we hug it out? Bygones and all that."

All the beings in the cell snapped into defensive stances. Seb's movement must have startled them. It wound the atmosphere so tight he could almost feel the air crackle. It could go one of two ways. Maybe he could front it out. Maybe they'd beat him to death. Still, it had to be better than getting infected with one of those damn parasites.

The edges of Seb's world blurred, his gift threatening to take him over. He drew deep breaths to ride it out for as long as possible. Regardless of what his dad had said, sometimes you had to fight. When you had just one path in front of you, you had to take it.

Two clenched fists, the cold spread of the steel running through the backs of his hands, and Seb snapped his head from side to side to loosen his neck up. He'd fight them and they needed to see that.

Although Seb stared at the mandulu on the other side of the cell, he'd have to get through the others first.

A tight jaw and Seb looked at the large brute with the cat eyes. Its chin stood out to him, daring him to punch it. One whack and it would go down. One whack would probably knock it clean off its face.

The snap of the lock on the cell door startled Seb. He spun around with his fists raised, expecting to see an attack from one of the other prisoners. When he saw the others look the same way, he lowered his guard before the door opened.

Although most of the inmates looked at the cell door, Seb saw the beast with the cat eyes and the mandulu in the corner hadn't. They both continued to glare straight at him.

The creatures close to the door backed away as three guards entered. Different than the ones who'd led Seb over there, yet they all held electric prods.

One of the prisoners looked to be carrying a leg injury. It shuffled to get out of the way, but it moved much slower than the others. One of the guards helped its retreat by prodding it. A loud crackle and the beast got flung into the wall in front of it. It spasmed as it lay on the ground, and all the other beings moved away from the guards quicker than before.

Once they'd cleared a space, their electric poles facing outwards at the prisoners, a fourth guard came in. He walked into the area they'd cleared and placed a bucket of swill on the floor in the middle of the room. He then pulled a stack of plates from a pouch in his dirty apron and placed them down next to it.

No more than seven plates, Seb looked at the creatures gathered there. Something would have to give when they tried to eat. Another glance at the mandulu in the corner and Seb saw the beast continued to stare at him. Something would have to give.

CHAPTER 6

The first one to approach the food left by the guards, Seb felt the stares from every being in the cell. The only sounds were his footsteps as he walked towards it. He didn't look at the others; he chose to focus on the slop in the pot instead. He picked up one of the limited plates available and moved towards the bucket of swill. Somewhere halfway between brown and green, the liquid looked like sick. But he had to eat first. An alpha display, it would keep the other prisoners off his back.

The room seemed to collectively hold its breath as Seb leaned down to spoon the swill onto his plate. Before he could grab the utensil, the mandulu broke the near silence.

"I wouldn't do that if I were you."

Seb took his time, milking the attention as he stood up and stared at the creature on the bed. He finally said, "If you were me, you wouldn't be bothering me at all. You'd realise the grave mistake you were about to make and you'd keep your fat mouth shut."

Instead of replying, the mandulu got to his feet and Seb's

world slipped into slow motion. It had to happen sooner or later. Better to initiate it than get sucker-punched when he lowered his guard.

The mandulu's actions sparked the large creature with the yellow cat eyes. It rushed at Seb first, coming at him in his left periphery.

Before it could get close, Seb threw his newly acquired plate at the beast. It spun through the air, and because he watched it in slow motion, he saw the brute's nose sink from where the rotating projectile impacted it. Not a definitive blow by any stretch, but it did enough to stun the creature, who blinked several times and shook its head.

The creature wiped its face and checked for blood. Seb took his opportunity and backed into the corner of the room again, leaning against the walls so they could only come at him from the front.

The cat-eyed creature rushed forward for a second time, the hard cell floor vibrating with its heavy steps. It had both of its large fists clenched.

A bone china chin, Seb lunged forward to meet it. He threw a cross with his metal right fist and caught it square on its weak spot.

It had been the first time he'd punched living flesh with his new fists. The creature's face buckled beneath his strike with a loud crack. In the short moment of contact, it felt like he'd turned the brute's chin to powder. Had the beast not fallen backwards, out cold, it would undoubtedly be screaming.

"Damn," Seb muttered to himself as he looked at his next attacker, his hands tingling with the desire to heal the one he'd just dropped. He had to learn to use his punches with a little more restraint.

The next creature looked similar to Bruke, but instead of green scales, it had a body covered in brown fur. A broad chest and thick arms like his friend, the beast could clearly punch when it needed to.

At first, Seb didn't see the creature's weak spot. It swung for him and he ducked. When he dropped level with its knees, he saw where he needed to hit.

Seb drove both fists forward together. Each one cracked against a kneecap. A pop ran through the space and he felt the snaps in response to his blows. He had shattered both patellas.

The creature crumpled in front of Seb, screaming as it reached down for its knees before pulling itself into the foetal position. At least he hadn't killed it. The buzzing desire to heal grew stronger in his palms.

Three mandulus rushed Seb next. They must have been the king of the cell's personal guard. They came forward as one, their heavy steps running a vibration through the hard floor like the cat-eyed creature had.

Like every mandulu Seb had ever met, they had large and weak chins, and he could see their punches coming from a mile away. He'd never understood how they considered themselves a warrior race.

A three-step dance to avoid each of their blows and Seb dropped one after the other in quick succession. He punched hard enough to crack jaws, but not so hard he'd kill them. No one needed to die to learn a lesson; at least, he hoped they didn't.

The pile of bodies mounted, yet seven more creatures rushed him. None of them seemed to learn from the lessons he'd already handed out. The seven looked to be some kind of crew, used to fighting together. Mismatched, they came at him at all heights. Two of them had wings and flew at him; three were so small they went for his shins.

Kicks to each of the little ones sent them all flying away. Seb ducked the fliers and knocked out the other two coming at him at his level. Again he showed restraint, punching one in the shoulder—clearly shattering its bones—and driving an open palm into the sternum of the other. Both fell down and didn't look like they'd get back up again.

With five down and the two flying, bat-like creatures buzzing around his head, Seb grabbed both of their legs and launched them into the far wall of the cell. They both hit it and slid down it like wet sponges.

Half of the cell defeated, Seb panted for breath as he waited for the next attack. None came.

Seb stared at the mandulu and the mandulu stared back at him.

The mandulu then rushed forward.

Only wanting to teach it a lesson, Seb stepped into the middle of the cell to meet it. He hit it across the chin with an open-palmed slap. The crack of his blow rang through the space and stung his palm. Better to go backhanded next time, he had no feeling there.

The fat-chinned brute fell away from the blow and landed limp on the hard ground like the others had.

After he'd watched it for a few seconds, Seb spun on the spot to take in the rest of the beings in the cell. "Anyone else want a go?"

Every creature he stared at looked away. He'd made his point.

At least he thought he had.

When Seb looked at a small grey creature no taller than about three feet and with long black hair, he saw it stare back at him. Before he could ask what it was looking at, the small being nodded behind him.

Seb spun around to find the mandulu back on its feet. It had its fists clenched, and before he could react, the creature swung for him.

After ducking its blow, Seb came up behind it and grabbed the back of its collar. Although he could have shattered its chin with one punch—and maybe he should have, he pushed on the back of the mandulu's fat head and forced it down towards the metal toilet in the middle of the cell.

A loud *clang* responded to the beast's face hitting the chrome bowl. The smell of countless creatures' shit wafted up from the dented toilet. Brown sludge exploded from it and coated the mandulu's face. The large brute fell away from the impact and lay limp on the ground.

Seb stood over it for a second, shoving its face with his foot. Definitely unconscious this time.

Silence swept around the place as Seb leaned down, picked up a plate, and spooned some of the slop onto it. He looked at the creature with the long black hair and winked. Pretty sure no one saw it, he stayed away from it so it didn't get into trouble with its peers. Snitches got stitches.

Seb walked over to the bed the mandulu had occupied and sat down on it. For a second, he watched the other beings, waiting for a challenge to him. When none came, he relaxed a little.

The rancid smell of curdled milk sat on Seb's spoon when he raised it to his lips. That should have been enough to warn him off, but he still poked his tongue out and dipped it into the slop.

The bitter tang lit up his taste buds like battery acid, sending a spasm through his tongue and forcing the muscles in his face to twist at the sharp kick. He threw the plate away from him. It hit the unconscious mandulu, the brownish, greenish swill mixing with the fecal matter it currently had on its face. Hard to tell where one ended and the other began.

The silence in the cell remained as the creatures formed an orderly queue to get their food. Incarceration had clearly trained their stomachs to tolerate it.

CHAPTER 7

An hour had passed, maybe two. During that time, Seb remained on the soiled mattress of the mangy bed in the corner of the cell. Springs poked into him wherever he distributed his weight and he itched all over. The bedbugs could have been a figment of his imagination, but figment or not, he itched all the same.

In any other situation, Seb would have moved away from the rotten bed. But to do that could concede his dominance in the space. Most of the beings he'd knocked out still lay on the cell floor. One of the two bat-like things had recovered, but other than that, they all remained unconscious. But beings could forget their place quickly, and one of them might get brave after they'd recovered. If they sensed weakness, they'd be on it in a flash. It definitely ruled out healing any of the creatures too, his hands itching with the desire to help them now he'd knocked them out.

At present, all the other beings in the cell remained relatively quiet. Other than breathing, flatulence, and a whole host of alien sounds that signalled rest for the different species, they said nothing.

Seb looked across at the small grey creature with the long hair. Would he have come a cropper if it hadn't given him a heads-up? Hard to tell, but it certainly helped to be warned about the mandulu behind him. Not that he could thank the creature more than he had already; he didn't want to make it a target for the others.

The slap of thick, leathery wings cut through the restless quiet in the cell. A look over to the corner of the room and Seb saw the other bat creature struggling to pull itself upright. It twisted and turned as if intoxicated.

When it opened its eyes, groggy at first, a confused frown dominated its dark grey face. Then it saw Seb and its eyes flew wide. The creature shifted backwards. It hit the wall and continued to press into it, its little clawed feet scraping against the cell's hard floor, sending a scratching sound around the space.

"Remember," Seb said as he watched the beast panic, his words pulling the attention of every creature in the room onto him, "*you* attacked *me*. I have no beef with you. As long as you don't come at me again, you won't get hurt."

The creature blinked several times. Its small chest rose and fell with its quick breaths. It finally settled down and nodded at him, although it still viewed him through narrowed and suspicious eyes.

Before Seb could say anything else, a sharp *crack* ripped through the room. When he turned to look at the cell's door, he noticed everyone else do the same.

A beast of a creature, Moses filled the doorway and glared at Seb. Many of the beings close to the leader of the Shadow Order shifted away from him.

For a second, Seb stared at Moses and said nothing.

"Don't make me ask you to come over," Moses said.

Seb still didn't move. "I can hear you from here."

The usual moment of silence followed in reaction to Seb saying something that displeased him. His jaw already wide, Moses clenched and unclenched it, the sides of his face thickening and relaxing with the action. It looked like he imagined chewing through Seb at that moment. Lustful hunger sat in his dark glare. Those jaws would probably make light work of a human body. Not that Seb would ever give him the chance.

A look down at the unconscious prisoners and Moses shook his head with a sigh. "Making yourself at home, then, I see?"

"Yep." Seb grinned. "I'm quite enjoying it in here." As he moved on the bed, a series of springs jabbed into him and he did his best to hide his discomfort.

"So you want to stay here permanently?"

Seb couldn't help but smile to see some of the prisoners tense at Moses' suggestion. They didn't want him there; it meant they'd have to keep a lid on themselves and stop behaving like morons. "It seems like the best option available to me at the moment."

A glance down at the mandulu Seb had knocked out against the toilet and Moses ruffled his large snout. "You like the smell in here? And the food?"

Now he'd spent a small amount of time in the cell, he couldn't smell it anymore. The food, on the other hand ... his stomach tensed to think of the rancid taste. "I know what you're doing."

A cocked eyebrow and nothing more. Moses continued to watch him.

"You're trying to make it as bad as you can for me in here so I do what you want me to do. But you forget, I've seen that footage you showed us. Things would have to be a whole lot worse in *here* for me to go *there*."

A shrug of his broad shoulders and Moses said, "Okay."

"Okay?" He didn't have anything else to say?

At that moment, Moses moved out of the door frame. It let a lot more light in and showed Seb the corridor beyond. The breath left his lungs. "Bruke? What's he doing out there? Where's he going?"

He walked with a line of Shadow Order soldiers. Reyes led the line. "Isn't that the girl from the mech suit?" Seb said. "The one who barely knows how to pilot one and probably couldn't tie her own shoelaces under pressure? The one who's here because of a favour to Daddy rather than because of what she can actually do?"

The now familiar predatory grin spread across Moses' face. He'd won and he knew it. "Bruke's off on another mission while we wait for you to decide what you want to do. And yes, that is the woman you fought in the mech suit. And I can tell you, she's not got any better. Hopefully she can look after your friend while they're out in the field. It would be such a shame to see him die."

It hurt to push off from the soiled mattress, the springs poking into the palms of Seb's hands. He moved over to the door, close enough to Moses to smell the fishy reek of him. Close enough to see the gruesome details of every white scar on his thick grey snout. "Why are you sending him out on a mission? And why with her? She's just a kid."

"He's joined the Shadow Order, Seb. I thought you already knew that? We feed, pay, and give him somewhere to stay. But we're not a charity. As a Shadow Order member, he has to work for us. I wouldn't worry though. The stuff Reyes has already survived, I'm sure she'll be fine. Although, there was that one mission she led a team back from where over half the crew died. But a fifty percent chance of survival is better than none, right?"

Seb shook his head. "You're lying. You're not sending that lot out."

"Maybe I am lying," Moses said.

Heat rose up Seb's neck in a tingling rush and spread through his face. He shook his head. "You're lying to me."

When Moses didn't reply, Seb looked from him to the disappearing Bruke. How could he ever forgive himself if Bruke didn't return?

Another look at the fat, scarred head of his boss and Seb let the tension fall from his body with a sigh. "Damn you, Moses."

It didn't look possible before, but Moses' smile spread even wider. It turned his large head into ninety percent teeth. "Are you ready to go back to work?"

A shake of his head and Seb dropped his attention to the ground. "Damn you."

CHAPTER 8

Tension wound tight in Seb at Moses getting one up on him. So when someone from behind him grabbed his arm, he turned on the creature, his fist raised and his teeth bared.

When he saw the grey being with the long black hair, he relaxed a little. "You?"

The creature shook in the face of Seb's fury. Its voice warbled. "Take care of yourself, Chosen One."

In that moment, Seb forgot about Moses and Bruke. So when the large creature snorted, sending a waft of fish forward, he spun around and glared at him. He then turned back to the grey being.

It encouraged the creature to continue. "You have something important to do. Much more important than the money-making missions he's sending you on." The creature looked at Moses before returning his attention to Seb. "Make sure you look after yourself."

Seb could already see the beings closing in around them. By talking so openly to him, the grey creature had risked its life. A weary acceptance sat in its humble stare. It had clearly been important to it to pass the prophecy on.

When Seb looked towards the cell's door, two guards had moved in front of Moses and raised their electric poles. The flicker of blue light strobed through the small room. "Steady on," he said to them. "I'm coming peacefully, just hold on a minute, yeah?"

Seb turned and looked at the others in the cell. "If I come back from my mission and anyone has harmed this creature, I'll make every one of you pay. Trust me."

It seemed to be enough to relax the tension in the room and the other prisoners stepped back. Seb turned to the grey creature again. "Why did you call me the chosen one?"

Eyes the colour of granite like the rest of him, the beast looked at Seb and wrung its hands. It stammered when it said, "B-b-b-because you are."

No more than he'd already been told, Seb said, "I've heard about the prophecy already, but how do *you* know about it?"

"We just know."

A firm grip on Seb's arm pulled him towards the door. Before he'd spun around, his world had slowed down. He saw the blue flicker of the prison guard's pole.

Cattle prod or not, Seb continued to spin around and drove a strong cross into the creature's chest. The guard might have been taller and heavier than him, but he still fell to the hard blow. They all fell if you knew where to hit them, especially when you had fists of steel.

After he'd watched the creature crumple, Seb turned back to the grey-skinned beast.

It reached up and grabbed both of Seb's hands, its eyes widening as it said, "Fulfil your potential, Chosen One. Use your gift."

Seb caught the rush of another prison guard in his peripheral vision. Before it could get to him, he spun around and drove an uppercut into its nose. The wet squelch of his metal fist crushing cartilage snapped through the room and the beast fell back, dropping its electric pole on the guard that had already been knocked out.

For a second, Seb watched the first guard twitch and convulse as electricity ran through it. The smell of singed hair came off the beast. Seb ruffled his nose at the stink before Moses stepped forward and kicked the pole away. Several creatures in the cell avoided its spinning trajectory.

Moses glowered at Seb, his patience clearly running out.

"Just give me a few more seconds, okay?" Seb said.

Moses didn't respond, so Seb turned to the grey creature. "Do you know anything about my mother?"

The creature shook its head. "No."

Frustration balled in Seb's tense body, but what could he do? The creature looked like the kind of being to tell him if it knew any more. "Okay," he said, and dipped a bow of appreciation. "Thank you." And with that, Seb left the cell, stepped over the unconscious guards, and followed Moses away from there.

CHAPTER 9

After spending a few hours in the prison cell, it felt great to be back with the others. SA and her grace, Sparks and her wit, Bruke ... Seb looked at Bruke at that moment to see the same anxious look he'd seen several times before on his green face. Not that he could blame him; they'd all seen the CCTV footage of what they were about to head into. But at least Moses hadn't sent him on a death-wish mission with Reyes. She wouldn't have been able to protect him like Seb could.

As much as Seb disliked the Shadow Order and their immoral approach to everything, they were his best option at present. A private firm had one motivation: profit. He might not like that, but it was the way of the universe, and until he'd done enough work for them to walk away, he had to accept it.

Besides, as he stood in the middle of the blaster section in their weapons warehouse, he couldn't help but be impressed. Big-paying jobs meant the Shadow Order had every weapon in the galaxy and they were all at his disposal.

Although, when SA wrapped two harnesses loaded with knives around herself, Seb forgot about the weapons and stared at her instead. The strapping hugged her lithe form like wet fabric. It took for her to stop and look back at him before he realised he had his mouth wide open as he stared at her.

Seb closed his mouth so quickly it made the slightest *clop* sound in the hard metal room. "Um," he said and shook his head to himself. A deep breath of the cold, metallic-scented air and he looked at the floor. Even in the frigid space, prickly heat rushed up his neck and smothered him. Could he have been any more blatant about it?

Because he didn't know where else to look, Seb turned his attention to the wall of blasters in front of him. He heard Sparks giggle, but he ignored it.

The room had just three walls. Instead of a doorway to access the space, the entire back wall had been removed to allow the room to open up into the larger warehouse. Every inch of the three remaining walls had blasters covering them. Seb saw every gun he knew existed and many, many more.

"I can't believe how many blasters they have," Seb said, loud enough for his voice to echo away from him into the larger warehouse behind.

"Not that we can use them in the third section of the complex," Sparks said. Her eyes widened. "Not unless you want to incinerate us all."

Seb shrugged. "There is that."

Bruke let out an anxious whine in response to Sparks' statement, but the others ignored him.

Sparks had her computer in her hands and most of her attention on the screen. When she looked to see Seb watching her, she turned the screen around to show him. "I'm downloading the schematics for the mining facility."

Seb didn't understand the mess of lines on the screen, so he didn't reply. Silence filled the space again and he returned to the shame of being caught gawking at SA. He hugged himself for warmth and spoke before he drowned in his embarrassment. "Why do you think it's so cold down here?"

Not looking up from her screen, Sparks said, "They probably have some highly volatile weapons somewhere. Raise the temperature too much and Aloo will turn to dust when they go off."

Before they could say anything else, Moses entered the room. He had four black radiation suits with him, all of them the correct size for each of the Shadow Order members. After he'd handed them out, he looked at the quartet, addressing them with his detached monotone. "You'll need these suits when you land and take off. If you go outside at any point, make sure you're wearing one. If you don't, it'll take just seconds for your skin to blister and your eyes to melt. Although, I'd strongly advise against going outside anyway. It's not a good idea on Carstic."

Not a whine this time, but Bruke shifted his weight from one foot to the other as if the ground beneath him had grown too hot to stand on.

Seb felt nervous too and drew a deep sigh that did nothing to calm the churning anxiety inside him. They were going into hell, but currently, hell seemed like his best option. He stepped towards the wall of blasters and pulled a semi-automatic from the rack. A two-handed weapon, he gripped its cold metal frame to test its weight.

When Seb turned around, he found SA watching him and instantly flushed hot again. Were it not for the biting air conditioning, he would undoubtedly be sweating at that moment. Why couldn't he keep his cool in front of her? He'd known her long enough now.

Seb forced a laugh to break the awkward silence. "I know Gurt would be disgusted to see me pick such a crass weapon. It's hardly the single-shot blasters he'd use. But we all know I can't shoot like him. I need to be able to spray blasts to give me any chance of hitting anything."

"Just make sure you don't hit me in the crossfire," Sparks said.

"You don't need to worry about that. Unless I'm trying to kneecap someone."

Sparks stuck out her long tongue at him.

Bruke still didn't speak. By the look on his green face, he seemed close to vomiting.

Because Bruke hadn't done anything since they'd entered the weapons room, Seb walked over to him and said, "Which one do you want?"

Bruke looked like he'd forgot how to talk.

When Moses tutted, Bruke's frown deepened as he clearly grew more anxious.

Seb moved over to the blasters and got another automatic rifle like the one he'd taken for himself. He held it in Bruke's direction. At first, Bruke stared at it and didn't move. "Come on, you're better having a weapon than not having one."

Bruke took the blaster with shaking hands.

"We're going to be fine," Seb said to his friend. "We'll land on Carstic, take out those parasites, and be back in time for dinner."

Silence swept around the room. Not even Moses got behind that statement, despite it being in his best interest to.

"Right," Moses finally said. "You lot need to suit up. We need to get you to Carstic."

Seb raised his eyebrows at Bruke. Bruke finally nodded back and picked up the suit Moses had dropped in front of him. They wouldn't be back in time for dinner, Bruke knew that, but Seb could see it felt better for him to pretend at that moment. Sometimes you needed to tell yourself lies to keep going. Sometimes the reality didn't bear thinking about.

CHAPTER 10

The shuttle shook and wobbled as they entered Carstic's atmosphere, blurring Seb's vision when he tried to look at the planet they were heading for. They still had a way to go, despite the large red expanse of wasteland dominating the view for some time now.

They all wore their black radiation suits. Although, at present, they sat with their visors open. They weren't close enough to need them closed yet. The thick suit restricted Seb's movements, it smelled of rubber and a hint of glue, and a layer of sweat stood out all over his body. But if it stopped him getting microwaved on Carstic, then it would be worth it.

From the second it came into view, Seb had been unable to take his eyes from what looked like a scorched planet beneath them. The closer they got to it, the more he questioned his decision. The prison cell had been a far better choice, but could he have let Bruke go with Reyes? Maybe he should have called Moses' bluff. They weren't going anywhere. But the consequences would have been too great to risk it. He looked at Bruke. The green-scaled creature sat on the hard metal bench with his eyes closed.

The mission felt pointless. They were about to risk their lives so Moses could get richer. Sure, they'd all receive a healthy bonus for it, but credits seemed much less important to Seb than they had in the past. He thought about what he used to be and shook his head. He'd fight in the pits for a small purse, rest for a couple of days, and do it all over again. Had he moved very far away from that with his new life? At least he knew the pits; he understood them and knew he would walk away unharmed. Hell, he even enjoyed the battles in the arenas. Another look at the red planet and he shuddered. It seemed more hostile than even the most volatile of crowds.

Would it have been better had Moses not told them anything? Now that Seb knew about the radiation, infection, and parasites, of course he felt apprehensive. "We need to get in and out as quickly as possible."

It took for Bruke to whine for Seb to realise he'd said it aloud. He clapped a hand to his mouth and mumbled, "Sorry, Bruke." After sharing a glance with SA, he added, "I was thinking that we need to make sure we're as efficient as we can be. Carstic's far from a holiday resort. It's not somewhere we want to hang around."

For the entire journey, Sparks had fiddled with her computer. When she finally looked up, Seb flicked his head in her direction. "Have you got a high score yet?"

"I'm not playing computer games." Sparks scowled at him. "If you must know, I'm making sure I have all the floor plans sorted before we go in there. Better to be prepared, eh?"

A nod and Seb said, "Jolly good. Keep it up." Whenever he felt nervous, he behaved like an idiot. Although aware of it, he couldn't do anything to change it, his mouth just ran away with him.

Before anyone else spoke, the monitor on the back wall of

the shuttle burst to life. A bright glow as the screen flickered for a second, and then a close-up of Moses appeared.

Seb flinched and pulled his face back. "Urgh!"

As he always did, Moses fixed Seb with a cold glare and said nothing.

"I'm sorry, big man." Seb laughed. "I wasn't expecting such an extreme zoom. I hate to break it to you, but you ain't the prettiest."

"I'm just here to reiterate," Moses said, ignoring Seb's dig. "We expect you to land, get into the mining complex, flush out all those bloody parasites, and get the hell out of there. There are plenty of ships in the hangar, so you should be able to get yourselves off the planet. However, if you don't manage that, we'll have a shuttle on standby. You got that?"

Nods moved around the shuttle and Seb gave Moses a thumbs-up and a wink.

"Oh, and Seb, I forgot to tell you; I give everyone three lives. Two warnings and you strike out on the third. Consider the nonsense with your refusal to go on this mission as your first warning."

"So I've got one more life to use?" Seb asked.

"Or don't use it at all," Moses said.

"And what happens when I've used all my wishes up? Do you go back into your lamp?"

After a deep sigh and exhale that pushed his thick cheeks out, Moses said, "Just watch it"—he then made quotation marks with his thick fingers—"*Chosen One.*"

Before Seb could say anything else, the screen turned black. Probably a good thing; he didn't know when to stop at the best of times. When he got such a favourable reaction from Moses, he found it even harder.

Seb looked at the other three to find them all staring at him. "What?"

"Why do you keep pushing him?" Bruke asked.

"Because it does him good to be challenged once in a while. We all need a challenge, right?"

"And what was he talking about when he called you Chosen One?"

Seb and Sparks looked at one another before Seb shrugged it off. "Never mind that. Hey, pilot," he called out, "are we there yet?"

"About fifteen minutes," the pilot shot back at him.

Seb turned his attention to Bruke. "I can't handle sitting here in silence for any longer. Why don't you tell us a little bit about yourself? We know you fight like the devil when pushed. What else is there to you?"

"I dunno," Bruke said as he rested back into his seat. "What do you want to know?"

"Why don't you have any family?" Sparks asked.

The same rage Seb had seen in Bruke's dark eyes on the battlefield returned and he clenched his thick fists. A set jaw and gritted teeth, he spoke in a low growl. "The Countess got them."

Were it not for the rattle and wobble of the shaking shuttle, there would have been silence in the back of the vessel.

Bruke finally continued. "I knew what she did to children when they reached twelve and older; everyone did. I didn't want to have to slaughter my family, so I ran away. If I wasn't there, they couldn't make me kill them, right?"

Seb nodded and the others continued to watch Bruke.

"But my neighbours sold me out. They must have told the Countess that my family had a boy of age. I would sometimes go past my old family home to check on them from a distance and make sure they were okay, but I noticed something wasn't right one time. When I checked the hut, I found my family dead inside." His eyes glazed as he stared into the middle distance. "They'd painted the word *deserter* on the wall with their blood."

A deep frown and Seb's pulse quickened. "What a thing to go through. I'm sorry. Did you ever find out who ratted on you?"

A shake of his head and Bruke looked down at the floor. "I would have killed them if I had."

When Bruke looked up, his brown eyes were glazed with tears.

Seb's heart sank. "At least we've stopped that from happening to anyone else, eh? You were an important part in overthrowing the Countess' rule."

A nod and Bruke said, "I was, wasn't I?"

"You may not have been able to save your own family, but you've saved thousands of families now. For that you should feel proud, even though I know it won't bring them back."

After he'd pulled a wet sniff in, Bruke nodded. "You're right. We have made a difference, haven't we?"

"And you know what?" Seb said. "Despite that greedy shark, Moses, we can carry on making a difference. He may be motivated by credits, but it seems that in the places we have to go to there are people that need our help. We can do that as well as fulfil our mission."

As much as he'd directed his comments at Bruke, Seb needed to remember that too. They *were* making a difference. They *did* help people.

The atmosphere in the shuttle had changed drastically. Maybe they all needed to remember what they were fighting for—they were rescuing a community, even if they were all dead. At least they could go in and deal with the parasites so no one else had to. And maybe there were some survivors. Moses' intel might not have been up to much.

As the shuttle continued to shake and wobble on its slow decline onto Carstic, Seb looked at the red planet in front of them again and pulled a deep breath into his tightening stomach. They needed to get in and get out. If they did that, everything would work out just fine.

CHAPTER 11

"We'll be landing in two minutes," the pilot—a lizard-like creature with feet for hands and hands for feet—called back at them.

A deep inhale to calm his rapidly accelerating pulse and Seb looked out of the front window again. He finally saw the mining complex. It stood as a large and ugly building in an otherwise barren landscape.

Seb pressed the button on the left side of his suit's hood and watched the visor slide across. It tinted his view of his surroundings with a yellow hue. It also altered the sound of everything. He still heard the rattle and shake of the shuttle, but the noises were toned down, muting them so he didn't have to be overwhelmed by them.

A look at Sparks, who'd just pressed her button, and Seb said, "If I'd known it would have been this much quieter with the visor closed, I would have pressed the button earlier."

Despite the yellow tint to his visor, Seb saw Sparks' nod just fine. The only slight distraction came from the radiation timer on the right of his vision. It read '3h', indicating how much time they had outside in Carstic's atmosphere before it became caustic.

When Seb looked at Bruke and SA, he saw they'd closed their visors too. The serene bioluminescent blue of SA regarded him with her usual level-headedness, a slight green tinge to her eyes because of the tint. Bruke's brown eyes were spread wide in his suit. The yellow didn't dilute his clear panic.

The shuttle suddenly dropped several metres, lifting Seb's stomach and forcing him to grab onto the barely padded armrests on either side of him. A shudder ran through the vessel that damn near rattled his teeth from his gums.

"The hangar's locked," the pilot called back. "I'll need to land outside and drop you off there. You'll have to find your own way in."

Seb looked at Sparks, who rolled her purple eyes at him before she said, "Never simple, is it?"

Another sudden drop and Seb's stomach flipped again. He craned his neck to see out of the front. They were just metres from the ground now. Although he tried to centre himself, he couldn't stop the adrenaline-fuelled shake running through him. They had three hours in their suits. Once they entered the complex, they didn't need to worry about radiation. They'd be fine. They had plenty of time, especially as they only had to open a door. Then Sparks' words repeated in his mind. *Never simple, is it?*

The shaking shuttle had been bad enough, but then it started swaying from side to side. Even with the muted sounds around him, Seb heard Bruke's whines and watched his friend grip his seat's handles. Were he less concerned about how he looked in front of SA, he might have done the same.

Another look out of the window and Seb clenched his jaw

to keep his anxious words in. They were heading at the planet like a meteor set to blow a crater in the rocky ground.

Seconds before impact, the shuttle suddenly stopped. Were it not for his seatbelt, Seb would have ended up in the front next to the pilot. Instead, the belt across his chest and waist took most of the jolt, ripping pains across his front from the sharp snap.

A low hum buzzed through the shuttle as it hovered for a few seconds before lowering the final few metres. The pilot pressed the button on the left side of his head and his visor shot across his face too. He lowered the exit ramp and called back to the team, "Good luck. Let us know if you need picking up."

"We won't need picking up," Seb said. "We have Sparks. She could pilot a rock out of here." He winked at his friend before unstrapping and getting to his feet. The radiation gear made it feel like he had a fat suit on. He picked up his gun on the way out of the ship and sped up to get off the shuttle before SA. Although she glared at him, she let him go. If it wasn't safe, he needed to be their first line of defence. He couldn't lose another friend.

Carstic looked as barren now that he'd reached it as it had from space. No signs of any life whatsoever. No small tufts of grass or weeds. No trees. No animal droppings, carcasses, or habitats. The hard, rocky ground looked scorched, although, surprisingly, it didn't feel hot like he'd expected it to. As flat as a runway, the horizon stretched for miles. Were it not for the large mining complex protruding from the ground, there wouldn't be anything but red rock.

As the others alighted from the shuttle, Seb reached up and took Sparks' hand to help her hop down. He did the same for Bruke. Clearly still pissed with him, SA came off last. Seb held his hand out for her and she simply stared at it before hopping from the shuttle with her usual grace. He couldn't help but smile at her.

The ramp pulled back into the shuttle. The entire thing rumbled with the engines powering up, and then it shot away from them back into the sky as if fired from a slingshot.

The sonic boom of it breaking the sound barrier made Seb jump as he watched it fly away. When it had vanished completely, he said, "Looks like we're on our own, then."

The mining complex had two huge chrome doors, which faced the group. The sun glistened off them, dazzling Seb even through his tinted view. It seemed impossible that such a scorched planet with such a bright sun wouldn't be hotter. Maybe Solsans had turned his blood cold and he didn't feel it as much. A shudder ripped through him to think about the dark and damp planet. If he never had to go back there again, it would be too soon.

"Right," Seb said, looking at the others lined up next to one another. "Everyone ready?"

Sparks had removed her backpack and pulled both of her blasters out. She held onto one and handed the other to SA before re-shouldering her bag then nodded at Seb. Bruke held his semi-automatic blaster and nodded too. SA stared at him.

"Okay," Seb said before he turned his back on them and led the way over to the hangar at a jog. Despite the muted sound through his suit, he heard the footsteps of the others following him.

The doors stood at least fifteen metres square. They would have let most passenger vessels in with ease. Up close, the building looked huge. In reality, it sat as a pimple on the vast landscape.

The timer changed on Seb's screen and dropped down to read '2h59m'. Only a minute, but his breathing sped up regardless. Something about the ticking clock put him on edge. But he wouldn't need his suit inside the complex; he had to remember that.

When they got to the building, Sparks walked towards the control panel by the massive doors. Seb went to one side of the structure so he could see past it. SA walked to the other side. Both of them had their blasters ready to fight should they need to. Not that Seb could see anything other than an endless expanse of red rock.

The sound of the wind on the vast plain ran through the speakers into Seb's ears, but the suit muted most of it. When he stepped a couple of paces away from the mining complex, a hard breeze pushed against him and sent him stumbling. The hangar must have shielded them from the worst of it when they'd disembarked the shuttle.

Sparks lifted her head from the keycard slot and called out, "The next area is free of gas."

"So we can use our blasters?" Seb asked.

"Yep."

Seb nodded to himself as he watched Sparks run several quick finger taps against her screen. The red light above the card reader turned green.

Just before Sparks pressed the screen to open the huge hangar doors, a deep thud banged against the other side of them. Even with his muted sound, Seb's heart kicked because of the loud crash. He watched the two doors shake from the impact.

A look at the others and Seb saw SA move close to Sparks. She dropped into a defensive crouch, ready for whatever would come out of the hangar at them.

After Seb had moved to the opposite side of the small Thrystian, his automatic blaster raised, Bruke joined them.

Another loud crash hit the other side of the doors. Seb turned to Bruke to see his face creased with a worried frown.

He put a hand on his friend's shoulder and said, "This is what we came here to fix. We were expecting this."

Several more bangs clattered against the doors.

Bruke stepped back half a step.

"Just follow our lead, okay?" Seb said.

Bruke nodded.

Sparks looked at Seb, her finger ready to press the open button. A deep breath to slow his world down and Seb turned to SA. She seemed ready. He turned back to Sparks and nodded. "Do it."

CHAPTER 12

Seb looked at the huge hangar doors and drew a deep breath. It did nothing to calm his hyperactive pulse. He watched Sparks point her long finger at the touch screen on her computer. One more ineffective inhale and he watched her press it.

The door's mechanism whirred. It added to the very few sounds around them. The wind, the whir, the banging of tens of hands.

With a dry mouth, Seb swayed from side to side to loosen up. He raised his gun, fitting the stock into his shoulder. Keeping one eye closed, he looked down the barrel at the crack running down the middle of the doors. The bright glare from the chrome forced him to squint. Were the sun any stronger, he wouldn't have seen anything.

As the crack opened, screams from what could have been hundreds spilled out. A deranged noise, it sounded like they were hearing themselves yell for the first time. They tested out the twisted undulations of their tormented cries. The quartet all stepped back a few paces.

Even with his world in slow motion, Bruke's shots surprised Seb. The scaled beast let out a high-pitched scream and fired on the slowly opening doors. Many of the green blasts crashed into the chrome barrier. Only one or two made it through the gap. At least that was what he guessed; it was hard to tell with the shower of sparks exploding away from each impact. It forced all four of them back a little more. Probably not a bad thing to get some extra distance.

When the doors parted wide enough, a sea of infected miners spilled out of the gap like guts from a split stomach. Radiation be damned, they flooded from the hangar unsuited.

The Shadow Order stepped back again as they opened fire.

Children, men, and women—they all wore the same twisted expression of rage. Of hate. Red eyes, twisted snarls, swinging arms. They slashed at the air, rapidly reducing the metres separating them and the Shadow Order as they charged. They had to be put down. Nothing could save them.

The line of monsters at the front fell to the blasts. The ones behind jumped them and kept coming forward. They didn't fear death. They didn't seem to even have a comprehension of it.

Even though ten were down already, about twice that amount pushed out through the ever-increasing gap behind them.

Seb blinked against the sweat running into his eyes. He had to stay focused. The blaster continued to shake with his rapid fire, the buck of it running through his entire body. But he kept the trigger down and blinked against the stinging saline trickle. He couldn't wipe it with his visor in the way.

Hot beneath the suit, Seb smelled his own funk and listened to the echo of his heavy breaths. A manifestation of his panic he couldn't ignore.

Then Seb's gun stopped working. Cramps ran through his trigger finger as he squeezed harder. Nothing. A look down at the top of his weapon and a red light glowed. It had overheated. "Shit!"

One of the infected miners rushed Seb. He tossed his gun to the ground when just a metre separated them. Red eyes, bared teeth, utter rage, she screamed the same demented scream he'd heard from all the others.

Seb punched her square in the face. The force of his metal fist buried into her. Even through the layer of radiation suit, he felt her nose turn to mush. It felt like her skull had cracked too.

As the creature fell away, Seb watched her in slow motion. A huge dent sat like a crater in her face. The rage in her eyes had gone. Any sign of life had gone. Blood ran from her mashed nose.

Bruke had also stopped shooting. His gun must have overheated too. Probably sooner than Seb's had on account of him shooting it first. Sparks and SA continued to rip off single shots into the creatures, but it wouldn't be enough to stem the flow of enraged bodies.

Because they were fighting humans, Seb saw the familiar weak spots on their chins and faces. Every punch he landed sank into their fragile bones. Each one threw back a nauseating crack. His new metal fists landed like bombs. It didn't matter that the suit restricted his movement, it looked like he had them beat.

A green blast then ran past Seb's face. He didn't even have time to flinch. He looked at SA, who had her gun pointed at him. He then looked at the infected miner she'd shot. A scorched hole sat in the centre of its furious scowl. He hadn't seen it coming.

The suit protected against radiation. However, not only

did it restrict Seb's movements, but it also created wicked blind spots where the visor didn't accommodate his peripheral vision. He looked back at SA and nodded thanks. Hopefully she'd have his back again if he needed it.

Five more miners, Seb rushed forward to meet them and dropped one after the other, barely breaking stride as he worked through them. Even though he had no feeling in his fists, he cracked skull after skull. Every blow turned another miner off.

It looked like they'd killed them all, but Seb still watched the gap in the hangar doors for more. Heavy breaths ran through him and he sweated harder than ever. Unable to wipe his face, the tickle of sweat ran torment against his skin.

"I think that's all of them," Seb finally said and picked up his gun. The red light had gone. It must have cooled down. He looked at the bodies of women, men, and children around him. They all lay limp on the red rocky ground. The timer on his screen read '2h57m'.

Seb continued to get his breath back as he walked towards Bruke. Of all of them, he needed the most looking after. His scaled friend stood frozen to the spot, breathing so fast his entire body rocked with his panic. "You okay?" he asked him.

But Bruke didn't reply, his wide eyes glazed as he stared into space.

~

BECAUSE OF BRUKE'S SIZE, SEB COULDN'T MOVE HIM. WHEN he tried to enlist the help of Sparks and SA, Sparks spoke for both of them. She suggested they let him recover on his own. Take him into the hangar in his current state and not only would he be useless to them, he'd be a hindrance. They'd potentially have to protect him as well as fight more of the things.

Seb looked at the reading on his screen, his anxiety manifesting as him bouncing on the spot. '2h50m'. Although he'd been trying to persuade Bruke to move for the entire time, he still continued to talk to his friend. "Come on, I know we have three hours in these suits, but I'd rather not waste it waiting around."

Suddenly Bruke snapped to life, lifting his blaster and ripping off a shot at Seb's feet.

Seb's world slowed down again as the green beam flew at him. He jumped at the last minute to avoid it.

Where he'd stood only a moment ago, Seb now saw the fried body of one of the parasitic worms. Just a few inches long, it lay dead. After a look at the parasite, he returned his attention to Bruke. He opened and closed his mouth several times before he said, "Thank you."

Where there had been anxiety in his friend's deep brown eyes, Bruke now stared determination at Seb.

"See?" Seb said to him. "You're meant to be here with us. Without you, I wouldn't have even made it into the hangar. You just saved my life."

The frozen panic that had occupied Bruke lifted. He pulled his shoulders back and straightened his spine. After a curt nod at Seb, he said, "Shouldn't we be asking where the worm came from?"

Why hadn't Seb thought about it? When he turned around and looked at the dead miners, he saw the cheek of one of the kids bulge. It looked like he'd come back to life and moved his tongue. The tip of a grub then appeared through his pursed lips. Before it could get any farther out, Seb shot the kid in the face. He didn't need to tell the others what to do.

When he looked, SA and Sparks had raised their weapons again and stared down at the sea of corpses.

Another deep breath, another woeful attempt to stifle his anxiety, and Seb looked down the barrel of his gun, waiting for the rush of parasites.

CHAPTER 13

Sparks ripped off the next shot, burning a hole in the cheek of a fallen man.

Seb then grabbed the kid he'd blasted and dragged it away from the pile of bodies. "We need to move these ones aside so we know which ones still have parasites in them."

A green blast hit the face of a woman next to Seb. SA had shot her, so he dragged the woman away too. Were Sparks not so small, she might have been able to move the man she'd shot, but because she couldn't, he moved that one next.

While the other three shot the grubs, Seb took on the job of moving all the corpses. They couldn't leave until all the parasites had gone. The bugs might not have been able to survive Carstic's radiation, but they couldn't rely on that.

Shot after shot, the faces of each miner snapped from the blasts.

After she'd dispatched three in quick succession, Seb moved past SA and dragged all three bodies away.

Even Bruke found his aim, blasting the dead miners' cheeks whenever he saw movement.

CHAPTER 14

By the time they'd killed all the grubs, sweat poured from Seb. But he had to let it be, his suit preventing him from doing anything about it. His arms ached from the effort of dragging all the corpses aside. His hands still buzzed from the need he'd had to heal every one of them, even though the power to heal the dead had eluded him thus far.

Regardless of his fatigue, Seb walked into the massive hangar first. Not that he had any illusions of being an alpha male; those men always reminded him of primitive humans. The reek of their testosterone hung so thick around them it left an aftertaste on his tongue. But he wanted to put himself in the firing line first. The others seemed to defer to him as their leader, so he felt he should be the one taking the risks. He couldn't let anyone else die the way Gurt had, even if it did mean SA staring at him like she wanted to knock him out. A born leader, she clearly hadn't been shoved back often.

The echo of Seb's footsteps came back at him as he walked through the hangar. A huge warehouse of a space, it had brushed metal walls. Being dark grey, they must have had the lead lining Moses had talked about. The floor that stretched through the space was the same red rock as outside. Wherever the radiation came from, it couldn't have been the ground. It must have been airborne.

A large collection of vehicles were scattered around the space. Mostly ships and shuttles, but there were a few tanks too.

It made Seb dizzy to look up at the high ceiling. It stood a little taller than the huge double doors. Now he'd seen the inside of the space, he had no doubt the place could accommodate large passenger shuttles with plenty of room to spare.

Still only a fraction of the way in, Seb stopped. Bruke and SA walked up next to him and also stopped. They waited for Sparks, who went to the keypad to close the double doors.

Several quick taps and the large barriers started to close with a deep whirring noise, the acoustics in the hangar accentuating the baritone sound.

"At least they were right about there being plenty of ships," Seb said to SA and Bruke while taking in the vehicles available to them again. "We should be able to fly out of here when we're done."

Having only taken a cursory glance before, Seb now zoned in on a large black tank parked over to one side. Something about the vehicle fascinated him. As big as the shuttle they'd flown in on, it had huge chunky tyres instead of tracks. They looked rugged enough to chew into the red rock. The design, with the slight wedge shape to its front and wide spoiler on the back, looked like it was a vehicle built for speed.

At the other end of the hangar, Seb saw another large set of double doors. Although this time, the doors were built into the ground.

"I'm guessing that's where we're going," Seb said with a nod of his head. "Into the earth."

"A mine's not going to be in any other place, is it?" Sparks said, her voice echoing from where she called over to him.

Bruke didn't speak. Instead, he shifted his weight from one foot to the other. Clearly anxious, but not as anxious as before.

The sunlight finally vanished, cut off by the closing of the huge hangar doors. A swirling rush of air buffeted the black fabric of Seb's suit and wobbled him where he stood. It didn't seem to bother SA. Bruke, on the other hand, spun around as if the elements were attacking him.

When the wind had died down, Seb saw Sparks look up above the hangar doors. He looked too and saw a large red light turn green. The radiation had been pulled out of the area. It had to be airborne like he'd thought.

As if to double-check, Sparks held her computer up, nodded, and said, "It's fine to take your suits off."

And not a moment too soon. Seb slapped the button on the left side of his head. His visor pulled away from his face and let in a fresh rush of air. It ran into his suit and cooled his hot skin.

Then the stench hit Seb as a wave of waste and rot. The parasite obviously curdled its host. It smelled like it turned them into festering bags of meat. Liver left to rot in the sun.

Seb heaved while he wiped the sweat from his face. When he'd recovered a little, he looked across at the others to see varying degrees of twisted disgust. "If it smells like this up here, what do you think it's like in the mines?"

The others looked at Seb, and Sparks spoke. "I think it's best we don't think about it."

Despite the reek, Seb still felt happier out of his suit than in it. He slithered free of the thick fabric, his surroundings brighter now he didn't have to look through the yellow tint of his visor.

Seb walked to the tank in the centre of the hangar and tossed his suit on top. The others copied him, although he had to help Sparks throw hers over the tall vehicle. When he smirked at her, she threw him a hand gesture that must have been an insult where she came from.

Another wipe of his brow did little to stem the flow of sweat. Seb pinched the front of his shirt and fanned it to help circulate the air. It brought him a little relief.

Bruke and Sparks looked as hot as Seb felt. SA, on the other hand, stood as a picture of cool serenity, as always. She looked around the space, her wide bioluminescent eyes taking it in.

"Right," Sparks said. "I don't know about you lot, but I want to get the hell out of here as quickly as possible."

She didn't wait for a response, instead walking over to the cellar doors leading down into the mines. And maybe the best way to deal with it; after all, they needed to get the job done. The more they thought on it, the more ominous the tunnels below the ground would seem.

The doors lay flush with the ground, and the keypad controls for them were on the wall next to them. Sparks looked at several keycards hanging from a hook. She took four and handed them out. Each had a lanyard, so they all dropped them around their necks like medals.

"These should make it easier to get through the closed-off sections," Sparks said. She then turned to the screen and hit a couple of taps against it. The green glow of it lit up her purple eyes and bounced off her glasses. "It looks fine down there. No gas leaks, and if there's no radiation up here, there won't be any down there."

"What about zombies?" Seb said.

The other three looked at him, but none of them spoke.

The ring of blades called out next to Seb and he turned to see SA had pulled out two of her seemingly endless supply of knives. They glinted under the hangar's strip lighting and she stared down at the double doors.

Although his second choice to his fists, Seb's gun gave him range, so he gripped the weapon tight and watched Bruke do the same. As he stared at the doors too, he listened hard. No sounds of infected humans on the other side. Maybe they'd cleared most of them out already. He laughed to himself. Yeah right, like it would be that easy.

"You ready?" Sparks said, her finger hovering near the panel to open the door.

Seb nodded, as did the other two. As ready as they could be.

Sparks pressed a button and the whir of the door's mechanism called out through the hangar.

CHAPTER 15

⤜⤛

"There aren't any zombies down there," Seb said as he peered into the dark pit.

"None we can see, you mean," Sparks shot back.

A look down into the gloom and Seb shrugged. "I was trying to be optimistic."

The hatch had opened wide enough to reveal the large square tunnel in the ground. Each of the walls spread about five metres wide. The doors that had covered the hatch weren't visible anymore from where they'd withdrawn into the rocks. A ladder as wide as each wall ran down them to the bottom. At least, what Seb judged to be the bottom. It was hard to be sure when he looked down into the murky depths of the hole.

Before anyone said anything else, a slight crack sounded out. Seb looked at Sparks to see her break a bright glow stick and drop it into the pit.

It seemed to take forever, the small strip of light spinning as it fell. The stick eventually stopped with a bounce at the bottom about fifty metres down. It lit up as a blue glow in the centre of the darkness. The shadows surrounding it looked utterly impenetrable.

Seb pointed down. "Did anyone else see that?"

Bruke didn't respond, looking from Seb to where he pointed and back to Seb again.

"What?" Sparks said.

"I thought I saw something move down there."

"You probably did."

"Well, that's helpful."

"Come on, Seb, we'd be kidding ourselves if we thought we'd completed our mission already. When is it ever that easy?"

What could he say to that? "Okay," Seb said, moving close to the edge of the hole. His stomach lifted to imagine the drop. "One of us needs to go down there."

Bruke stepped back a pace.

"If one of us goes," Seb said, "they can draw out whatever's waiting for us; then the others can shoot from up here. We're in a much more offensive position. It would be a shame to sacrifice that by all of us going down there together."

"So we'll use the person who goes down as bait?" Sparks said, one of her eyebrows raised.

Bruke moved back another step and shook his head. "I'm not going."

As Seb stared down into the hole, he watched the glow stick slowly die. The darkness appeared to overpower the blue light, snuffing out its spirit. Before Seb could say anything, Sparks returned to the control panel. After several taps, some lights flickered on down below.

Seb relaxed his taut frame. Everything looked better when lit up. The hole smelled of damp earth and gas, although only the faintest whiff of gas. "Is it safe down there for blasters, Sparks?"

Sparks ruffled her nose as she sniffed the air. "It does smell, doesn't it? Although, ruthane should be odourless. We could well be smelling the stuff they put into it so you know there's a leak."

After sitting down on the ground, Sparks let her legs hang down into the hole and leaned her computer into the space as far as she could reach. When she pulled it back out again, she stared at the screen for a second and nodded. "Yep, just as I thought, the smell is the agent they put into it to tell us there's gas down there. It's fine."

"You sure?" Seb asked.

"Would I be risking it if I wasn't?"

Seb accepted her point with a nod.

SA stepped towards the edge of the hole as if to go down there and Seb grabbed her arm. When she turned to him, she levelled the same rage she'd stared at him since they'd landed on the planet. He bowed at her. "I have massive respect for you volunteering, but I need to do this. I can't expect anyone else to go down."

She cocked her eyebrow and put her hand on her hip.

"Please," Seb said. "Let me do this." He couldn't let anyone else die.

The two stared at one another for a few seconds before SA stepped away from the hole. Although she'd accepted it, she looked far from pleased about it.

"Thank you," Seb said.

Too much more thought and he wouldn't go down there, so Seb climbed backwards onto the ladder, dropping a foot down onto the top rung first before lowering himself into the hole. The large bars attached to the wall were rough, cold, and speckled with rust.

A quick glance down into the pit behind him again and Seb's world spun. He stopped his descent and gripped on tight while he closed his eyes.

It took a few seconds, but he calmed down, his balance returning. It would be better if he didn't look.

Not a hard climb, but with a river of adrenaline rushing through him, Seb shook from the effort of his descent. One rung at a time, he climbed down into the poorly lit pit. Hopefully, if they had anything to fight down there, the others would hit them and not him when they shot into the hole. Whatever happened, he couldn't have let anyone else climb down. It had to be him.

CHAPTER 16

The air might have got cooler the farther Seb descended into the mine, but that didn't stop his body turning slick with sweat. A continued rush of adrenaline seemed to force every drop of moisture from him, and his lungs tightened with his panic. He gasped as he climbed.

Thankfully he'd been able to shed the radiation suit up above. If he'd had to make the descent in that thing, he wouldn't have coped.

Seb stepped off the bottom rung and fought to regulate his breaths. The smell of gas gave way to the damp reek of soil. Humidity hung so thick in the cold air, he couldn't be sure where his sweat ended and where it began.

Despite Sparks fixing the lights down in the mine, they didn't do the best job of illuminating the place. The picture Moses had painted of a modern facility stood a great distance away from the reality of where Seb found himself.

A tunnel, so basic that the walls were exposed soil, ran away from him. Loose wires linked single light bulbs, which hung from the ceiling by cords. The place looked like it belonged in the last century.

Just one bulb dangled down about every ten metres. They gave off a glowing splash, casting a circle of illumination on the muddy ground. Seb saw more shadow than he did light stretching away from him down the long tunnel.

The zombies could be anywhere. Although, despite his poor visibility, Seb could still hear well enough. At that moment, he couldn't hear anything other than the pound of his own pulse.

A look back up to the top of the hole and Seb saw the faces of his three friends staring down at him. They seemed impossibly high. Much too high for him to reach should he need a quick getaway.

As he looked at the three expectant stares, Seb shrugged. "It seems okay down here."

"You can't see any of them?" Sparks asked, her high-pitched voice echoing through the tunnel. If there were any down there, the sounds of their conversation would no doubt rouse them.

"I can't see much of anything down here. But from what I can make out, it looks to be clear."

"Shall we come down?" Bruke asked.

A shake of his head and Seb drew a deep breath. He spoke on the exhale as he said, "No."

Bruke looked confused, so Seb elaborated. "I think you should just wait up there for the entire time and let me handle this on my own."

A whine rode Bruke's words. "There's no need to be sarcastic."

"You know what, Bruke, sometimes there is. And when your standing fifty metres from safety in a dark mine that could be crawling with zombies, I would say this is one of those times."

Before Bruke could say anything else, Seb heard a sound

from the darkness far down the tunnel. At least, he thought he did.

"What is it?" Sparks asked, her voice hissing through the space.

"Can you shut up?" Seb said.

For a second, Seb's pulse beat louder than the approaching sound. Maybe he'd imagined it. But then it came again, a wet slapping sound of feet against the damp ground. Lots of feet. And they were moving fast.

CHAPTER 17

The shadow at the end of the tunnel sat so dark Seb couldn't tell whether he saw movement within it or not. Sure, the lights ran a long way back, but unless something passed directly beneath them, they'd be hidden in the blackness.

When the sound got louder, Seb looked up at his friends. "Can you hear that?"

"Yep," Bruke said, his voice shaking.

After just a few seconds, the sound swirled through the tunnel. It rushed at Seb like a tsunami. He'd be drowning in it before he knew it, yet he still couldn't see anything.

Seb squinted to try to see better, his gaze fixed on the farthest splash of light. He raised his blaster to his shoulder, closed one eye, and peered down the barrel of it.

The shadows at the end of the tunnel seemed to shift with the onrush of something. The inky void made it look like the darkness itself had come to life.

Seb held his breath, his pounding heart rocking his entire body. He squeezed the trigger, ready to let rip.

Any second and Seb would see them.

Then the farthest light went out as if the power had failed.

"Sparks!" Seb shouted, his attention on where the light had been only a second ago. "The lights are going out down here. Help!"

If the climb back up were half the height, then maybe Seb would have gone for it. Even then he would have questioned it. If he tried now, the zombies would catch him, drag him back and rip him to shreds. He had just one choice: stay and fight.

The next light flickered for a second and then blinked out too.

The scream of the zombies joined the rush of their heavy footsteps. Shrill and with a tittering staccato, the screamers sounded bat-shit crazy.

"Sparks!" Seb called again as he watched another light ping off. "What's happening?"

Before Sparks responded to him, every light in the tunnel failed.

The zombies screamed louder than before, invigorated by gaining an even greater advantage. They continued to come forward in a stampede.

Where Seb had smelled soil and the odour added to the gas, he now smelled the rotten reek he'd inhaled in the hangar. Festering meat, cloying and rancid.

He now felt the vibration of their feet through the damp ground.

It seemed as ineffective now as it had done the first time he did it. Still, Seb looked up at the three distant faces again and shouted, "Sparks! I need you to *do* something."

CHAPTER 18

The gun shook as Seb wrapped it in a tight grip, aimed down the dark tunnel, and clamped his finger on the trigger. It didn't matter that his world now moved in slow motion, the zombies were lightning, closing the space between them much quicker than he could repel their attack.

Green blaster fire lit up the tunnel, creating a strobe effect as every blast came to life and then died against the chest, lap, leg, arm, or whatever part of a zombie it hit. Some of the creatures fell away from Seb's blasts, their arms clipped, their heads blown off. Although, only some and nowhere near enough.

The green strobes of light were a poor substitute for poor lighting; however, they did show the wave of zombies getting closer with every second. They showed him that he couldn't beat them on his own.

The smell of gas had completely vanished. It had been replaced with the reek of rotten meat, halitosis, and the curdled stench of milk.

Seb glanced down at the top of his shaking gun. The green light had turned orange already. "Shit!" Maybe the others could hear him over the noise, maybe not. He had to try. "I'm about to overheat. Help me out down here."

A green blast crashed into the ground in front of Seb at the entrance to the tunnel. He jumped back from it. When he looked up, he saw Bruke with his gun in his hand. He quickened his retreat until his back pressed against the metal ladder rungs in the far wall. From the square of light from the hangar above, he'd see the zombies the second they entered it, so he stood as far on the other side of it as he could.

Another green blast splashed down at the tunnel's entrance. It didn't hit anything, but at least it helped Seb see better. The bright glow showed him the wave of creatures about to burst from the darkness.

One of Sparks' glow sticks landed where the others had shot. A small help. Very small. But Seb could tell how close the zombies were because the ground shook with their thundering onrush.

Several more glow sticks lit up in the mouth of the tunnel just as Seb's gun failed.

After he'd discarded his weapon, Seb raised his metal fists, screamed back at the first zombie to leave the darkness of the tunnel, and threw a punch into the centre of its face.

Steel connected with weak bone and Seb felt his hand sink into the creature's nose. For the briefest moment, he saw the human it used to be and the slightest tug of reluctance threatened to grind him to a halt. But when another one came at him, he punched it like he had the first. It fell away—out cold at least, probably dead.

Two more came at Seb as green blasts rained down from above.

Seb dropped them both. The others continued to miss. They'd have to do better if he was to get out of there.

One after the other, Seb dropped the beasts as they rushed

him, switching his mind off to what they used to be. They were monsters now and nothing more. They needed to be eradicated for the safety of others.

Maybe fifteen of them, maybe more, they all had the weak bone structure of a human, and all went down to his punches.

Were it not for the glow sticks and the flash of blaster fire from above, Seb wouldn't have been able to see them as early as he did. His team might not have hit the mark with every shot, but at least the green splashes of light at the mouth of the tunnel had some use.

Because Seb had stepped back so far, he had nowhere else to go. The thick rungs of the ladder pressed into him, and the creatures still rushed forwards. He yelled and continued to throw punches. For every zombie he dropped, two more replaced them.

Sweat ran down Seb's face, but he didn't stop to wipe it off. Wide mouths yelled at him and he punched them shut. Red eyes fixed on him and he knocked them away. Flailing arms reached for him and he drove them back, each attack drawing slightly closer than the one before it.

CHAPTER 19

One thing about the world moving in slow motion was it dragged out every painful second of what were often very painful experiences. Maybe the battle hadn't lasted for hours, but for Seb, living it through his slowed-down perspective had made it feel like it had. Although, without it, he would be dead instead of the pile of zombies in front of him.

Other than the sound of his own exhausted breaths running away from him into the darkness, Seb couldn't hear anything else. He stood with his gun and watched for movement. As much as he'd wanted to leave his weapon on the ground because it had betrayed him twice now, it had cooled down and he needed something to shoot the parasites with when they emerged.

The air reeked of the curdled stench of the creatures, and up to forty bodies lay dead at Seb's feet. Forty bodies of what were once people. Forty bodies that would soon give up the parasites inside them.

Seb's eyes stung from not blinking as he watched the corpses. The ones outside the hangar had taken at least five minutes, but he couldn't rely on these taking as long to show their ugly little faces. Until he knew every grub had been eradicated, he had to remain vigilant.

Despite looking at a sea of human corpses, Seb had to think of them as monsters. He wouldn't complete the mission if he didn't.

The lights were still out in the dark tunnel. Maybe more zombies would rush from down there. From what Seb had seen, they didn't do stealth. Hopefully that would continue and he'd hear them coming from a mile away.

The sound of the others climbed down the metal rungs towards Seb. They moved quickly, clearly anticipating the emergence of the grubs too.

After a glance up at his teammates, Seb returned his attention to the corpses and the mouth of the pitch-black tunnel.

Although Seb had recovered his breath, he still sweated heavily. He wiped his arm across his forehead to stem the flow and help ease the sting in his tired eyes.

SA reached the bottom first, and then Bruke. Sparks, with her small legs, had only made it about halfway by the time the other two stepped off the ladders.

"Are you okay?" Bruke asked, looking Seb up and down as if a scan of his body would answer his question.

Seb shrugged and felt the attention of SA on him as if she'd also asked the same thing. At least she didn't stare contempt at him at that moment.

Bruke nodded at Seb's weapon. "Your gun overheated again?"

"Yeah, stupid things," Seb said. Thank god for his fists. He opened and closed them several times. Everything else felt tired, but his fists still felt brand new. Cold, but brand new. He smiled. "It was much easier with my hands. No overheating here."

Both SA and Bruke looked down at the corpses at the same time. "No grubs yet?"

A shrug and Seb offered, "Not yet. The waiting's the worst part. I just want to deal with them and move on."

When Sparks finally got to the bottom of the ladders, she stared down into the darkness and gasped. "How did you fight in this?"

"With great difficulty," Seb said, his attention still on the bodies. "We could do with the lights back on in case there are more zombies down there."

Sparks looked at the bodies before she moved away. Seb watched her light up a wall with the torch on her computer. It illuminated what looked to be an electrical box of some sort.

It took no more than a minute of her fiddling before the place lit up again. Although, the poor attempt at lighting would hardly qualify as lit up; it looked like it had before the electricity went out.

"I'm guessing the vibrations made by the creatures running up the tunnel tripped some faulty wiring somewhere. Hopefully it'll stay on now."

"Hopefully?"

"It's all I've got, Seb."

Even in the short time it had been dark for, Seb had forgotten just how far the tunnel stretched. He looked down the line of weak lights all the way to the farthest one. Maybe he should be grateful for what his blaster gave him. A shorter corridor with no projectile weapon, and he might not have been standing there at that moment.

The extra light helped Seb see the dead better; there were probably close to fifty of them. His heart rate increased to look at what he'd come up against. "I'm not sure I would have been as willing to fight if I'd seen just how many of them there were."

Before anyone could respond, the flash of one of SA's blades flew past Seb. It embedded in the mouth of one of the corpses.

Seb's world flipped back into slow motion.

Even though he'd seen it happen before, a shudder rolled through Seb to watch the grubs emerge from the bodies of the corpses. Although fast when free of their hosts, they looked to be struggling to get out. Slick and shining with what must be bile or some other internal fluid, they poked out through the lips of the cadavers.

A hard stamp on the head of the closest corpse and Seb crushed both the grub and woman's face beneath his boot heel. The pop of the small creature filled the air with the acrid stench of rot, a much more potent smell than the zombies had given off.

The others around Seb trained their blasters on the corpses. A second later, the small space lit up with a flurry of shots at the emergence of the grubs.

CHAPTER 20

By the time they'd killed every grub, the air hung heavy with the rotten stench of the vulgar little creatures. So rich, Seb heaved several times as he walked through the fallen bodies, the tight pinch he held on his nose doing little to prevent the reek from getting through.

Bruke had taken it upon himself to move the corpses to the side when they knew they'd definitely killed the parasites in them. It left a small group of five far down the tunnel, which Seb, SA, and Sparks shot full of holes.

"I think we got them all," Seb said, his arms aching from his gun's recoil. He led the way in, leaving the bodies behind, and moved far enough down the tunnel to get clear of their acrid stench.

The smell of the agent they added to the gas replaced the reek. The memory of the grub's tang still remained with Seb, but to put the pile of bodies behind them allowed him to relax ever so slightly. Despite what the people had turned into, they were humans at one time and he could only bear the pain of looking at them for so long.

Although Seb had travelled farther down the tunnel than

he'd been able to see from the bottom of the ladder rungs, it still stretched away from him into a seemingly never-ending darkness. The light bulbs worked, but they were still utterly ineffective at giving him any sense of perspective. God knew how far they had to venture before they reached the first section of the mining complex.

Seb waited for the others to catch up to him, and when they were all together, Sparks produced her small computer. The bright screen lit up the gloom. An image of a map dominated the device and she used her long index finger to point while she spoke. "This is where we are now. It's hard to tell when you look down the tunnel, but we're not very far from the living quarters. I don't think the state of this walkway is a fair reflection of what the dorms are like. I expect them to be more habitable, but we'll see."

"I hope you're right," Seb said as he looked around him at the bare soil and weak light bulbs. "The parasites would have done them a favour if this is how they were expected to live."

The looks from the others made Seb recoil. Probably not the most sensitive comment he'd made, but sometimes humour worked best. After all, he had just murdered about fifty people. If he didn't laugh … well … "Come on," he said and moved on.

"Moses was correct when he said this place has been divided into sections," Sparks said as they walked. "I still can't get any gas readings down here, so my guess is—if not all of the sections—that this one at least is sealed off from the rest of the place."

"So there could be more zombies down there?" Seb said. "Locked in the other sections, I mean."

A look at Seb and Sparks nodded. "I think we need to assume there could be zombies anywhere down here. But, to your question specifically, yes, I'd be very surprised if we don't get rushed when we try to access the next section."

Not that she'd just told him anything he didn't know, but Seb's heart still sank to think of another fight like the one they'd just had. Although, at least he wouldn't be on his own this time. "So what's in the next two areas?"

"This is where the people sleep," Sparks said, showing Seb her computer as they walked. She then pointed at the next section on the map. "This is the recreational area, the canteen, the sports hall, the games room." Her voice dropped when she pointed at the final section. "And this is the mine."

"No guns down there," Seb said.

"No guns, and maybe the biggest concentration of those grub things too." When Sparks looked up, the shine from her computer's screen cast disturbing shadows on her face, her eyes sunken by the appearance of thick bags beneath them.

Seb looked away down the tunnel and pulled a deep breath in. "One section at a time. That's all we should focus on for now."

Silence met Seb's comment.

While they'd been talking and looking at Sparks' computer, they'd slowed down to an almost halt. Reluctance had clearly taken hold of them. "Right," Seb said, clapping his hands and sending the sharp crack of it away from him down the tunnel. "I suppose we'd best pick up the pace, then, eh?" He looked at the others and they all nodded. None of them with any enthusiasm—yet maybe to expect any reached a bit too far. Before he lost all of his motivation, he strode off down the tunnel, his gun raised, his heart pounding.

CHAPTER 21

When they reached the next set of doors, it took all of Seb's will not to suggest they turn around. They could go back to the hangar, get a ship, and get the hell out of there. In reality, he knew they couldn't get away with it. There was no way they were getting off Carstic until they'd done what they'd been sent to do.

Sparks stepped forward and Seb grabbed her left shoulder, halting her progress.

A hard stare like she wanted to shoot him, she then shrugged him off. "Just trust me, yeah?"

Another look at the doors in front of them, down to his purple-eyed friend, and back at the doors, and Seb sighed. "Don't say I didn't warn you." He let go of her and raised his gun, watching the doors down the barrel of it.

When Sparks got close to the doors, they slid open, a bright glare of light spilling out of them.

Seb pulled his head away from his gun and looked at her. "Huh?"

It took for Sparks to point a long finger above the doors

for Seb to see it. A small plastic box with a pinprick of a red light on it. "It's a sensor."

Seb didn't respond.

"If the *zombies*, as you call them, got anywhere near these doors, they would have opened for them. Now, we can't be complacent because there might be some stragglers through here, but these aren't the doors to the next section."

Sparks stepped through the double doors and Seb sped up to follow her with the other two beside him.

"Wow," Bruke said when they'd all entered the place. "I wasn't expecting it to look like this."

A white floor, white walls, and a white ceiling. Strip lighting ran the length of the long corridor all the way to the double doors at the end. A chill in the air sent a shudder through Seb. "Sure, it's cold, but compared to that tunnel we just came down, it actually looks habitable."

Sparks pointed to the doors at the end. "They're the doors we need to worry about."

After he'd looked at them for a moment, Seb looked at the other doors running down one side of the illuminated corridor. Ten to fifteen of them, they were clearly the rooms the miners stayed in. "Right," he said. "Let's get this section cleared and move on. The sooner we get off this planet, the better."

The change from the exposed earth to the hard white floor made walking much easier. For the first few steps, Seb lifted his feet a little bit too high because he expected the ground to cling on to the soles of his shoes.

When they were close to the first door, Seb ruffled his nose. "What's that smell?"

"Bleach," Sparks said.

"What for?" Bruke asked.

"Just a guess," Sparks said, "but I'd assume they kept it disinfected down here to keep viruses and bugs out."

Seb snorted an ironic laugh. "Not that it worked."

The others looked at him and he shrugged. "Well, it didn't."

When they got to the first room, Seb used the keycard Sparks had given him in the hangar to swipe through the reader and open the door. It slid across with a *whoosh*.

As he entered the room, Seb pressed the stock of his gun into his shoulder.

A small space, the lights left no surprises like the shadowy tunnel had. It had three beds in it: one double and two singles. The singles were on one side of the room, the double on the other. All three beds were unmade.

"That one must have belonged to a teenager," Sparks said and pointed at one of the beds. A poster of a music band Seb had never heard of hung above it, a stack of books beside it.

When Seb looked at the bed next to it, his heart sank. He looked across to see the others were staring at it too. Although the same size as the other single bed, it had a crayon drawing above it instead of a poster. Done by a child of six or seven years old, it had a stick-figure family, a rainbow, a bright sun, and a dog. All the things that child would never have in the mines, save the family.

Seb sighed and swallowed against the lump in his throat. A stack of books lay next to the bed. They were the kind of books where the pages were made from card and they were filled with colourful pictures. The beginning of tears itched his eyes to look at them and he shook his head. "They didn't deserve this."

Silence.

To break the stillness if nothing else, Seb cleared his throat. "I'd say this room's clear."

It took for him to look at the others before Sparks replied. She spoke with a warble in her voice. "Yep."

Many of the rooms looked the same. Some had bunk beds for what must have been single men and women. Some were family rooms like the first one they'd visited. Every one showed a snapshot of the lives that had been lived in the mines. A snapshot of the lives that had been lost.

When they got to the last room in the corridor, SA tried to go in first, but Seb barged past her.

Six single beds and a double, Seb laughed to see them. It felt good to relieve the tension. "Wow, the parents must have been busy in this one. Although, I suppose on those cold and lonely nights—which must have been every night in this place—what else could they do but make babies?"

Seb looked at SA, only then realising it seemed like he'd addressed her directly. Heat smothered his face and he dropped his attention to the floor. "Um, I mean. Um, what I mean. Um …"

But something cut Seb off. The smell had been there all along—rot, rancid meat. It hung faint in the air, but he definitely smelled it. He should have caught it sooner.

A particularly messy room, Seb suddenly saw a pile of clothes in the corner shift. He raised his gun and looked down the barrel of it. The others did the same.

It started as a groan and quickly turned into a snake-like hiss. Angry, it sounded like whatever made the noise could and would bite.

Seb glanced at the others. They were all ready for this.

Where he'd expected something larger, Seb jumped back to see a child spring from the dirty laundry. His world slipped into slow motion as the angry little thing threw the sheets clear of herself.

Like the girl in the clip Moses had played them, she

looked to be between about eight and ten years old. She had the blood-red glare of the other zombies and stretched her mouth wide as if releasing a silent scream. She then snapped her mouth shut, clamped her teeth, and hissed again as she focused on him.

Just one zombie and the brightness of the room allowed Seb to feel calm enough to take her in for a moment. She had a damp lap at the front and was no doubt soiled at the back. The smell of waste stirred up with her movement.

Seb still hadn't pulled the trigger. It had been different when they'd been part of a crowd, but now he faced a little girl on her own. Now he'd seen what her life had been like, his finger froze. He couldn't do it.

To look at the girl's cherub face—chubby with puppy fat—showed just how little she was. But she'd gone and he couldn't do anything to stop it. Life had been cruel to her and he couldn't reverse that.

The others remained frozen as if waiting for him to do something. A clenched jaw and Seb winced, but he still couldn't pull the trigger.

Then the girl sprang to life. She jumped over the bed between her and Seb and launched herself at him.

Even in slow motion she moved fast. Seb yelled as he raised his gun, aimed it at her, and pulled the trigger. Although he closed his eyes, he listened to her take the shot and hit the floor.

It took a few seconds before Seb opened his eyes again and saw the girl on her back. Dead. A hole sat in the centre of her face and she stared up at the ceiling with a listless gaze. A twisted look of horror had frozen her features.

Silence hung in the air again before Seb said, "She didn't deserve that."

Sparks let go of a heavy sigh. "None of them did."

CHAPTER 22

Within a few seconds, silence swept through the family's room as if the air had been sucked from it. Everywhere Seb looked, he saw reminders of the lives that had been lived down there. Toys, books, drawings ... hell, he could almost hear their laughter ... their cries. The beginning of tears itched his eyes, but he couldn't get sentimental. Not now. He turned his attention away from the personal belongings in the room and looked down at the little girl's corpse again.

Although not easy, Seb found it easier to look at the dead child than anywhere else. At least the corpse didn't have a narrative of what it once was. Just a dead body; he didn't have to think about its past.

The other Shadow Order members stood beside Seb, but he'd killed the girl. Their gesture of solidarity didn't mean much to him at that moment. A fierce buzz ran through his hands from wanting to put them on the girl's wound. His hands still hadn't got the message. He couldn't resurrect the dead.

About five minutes had passed before Seb finally felt like

he could look up again without crying; he glanced around the room and stopped on the parents' bed. Unmade like most of the other beds, it suggested the grubs had attacked when a lot of the miners were sleeping.

The mine couldn't have been an easy place to raise six kids. Not that anywhere would be an easy place to raise six kids. Hopefully there had been enough grubs for them to all fall at the same time. It would have been awful if any of them had to watch loved ones get taken over like the girl in the clip Moses had shown them.

As the narrative of the place grew again in Seb's mind, he shook his head to try to shake it off. He still had to kill people. It wouldn't help to understand who they were before the parasites attacked.

Still no one spoke. Seb looked across at each of the others in turn, but none of them looked back at him, instead fixing their attention on the dead girl. The grub had to come out soon, so they had to wait. Hopefully they wouldn't have to wait too much longer.

Then Seb saw it. The slightest movement in her chubby cheeks as if she shifted her tongue around the inside of her mouth. A deep breath to settle his rampaging heart before he looked down the barrel of his gun at her. They'd never called him their leader, but when a tough decision or action needed to be made, it seemed that he had the broadest shoulders. Certainly no resentful looks from SA at that moment.

A gentle parting of her puffy little lips and Seb shook as he watched on. The end of his gun wobbled. Hopefully he wouldn't miss. The pointed tip of the grub's little body—slick and glistening with what must have been bile like he'd seen with the others—poked from her mouth.

Although he didn't look up, Seb felt the attention of the

others on him. It didn't matter what he felt like doing, he *had* to do this.

He pulled the trigger.

A kick of recoil bucked through the gun and a rancid shot of rot and cauterised flesh filled the small room.

Another hole in the poor girl's innocent face.

Seb stood up and turned his back on the tiny corpse. "Come on," he said, the others finally looking at him. "Let's get out of here."

From the response the others gave him, it seemed like Seb couldn't have said it soon enough. Bruke led the way to the door.

CHAPTER 23

The four left the room and walked the short distance to the double doors leading to the next section of the complex. The doorway stood large enough to drive a tank through, the closed doors forming a tight seal against any gas leakage.

Sparks walked over to the panel where the keycard should go and brought up her mini-computer.

"At least we've cleared out one section," Seb said to SA and Bruke. "Two more to go and we can get out of here."

When Seb saw SA looking at him, he looked back. From the way she stared at him, her deep and compassionate gaze looked like she wanted to tell him something. Maybe he'd misread it, but it felt like support of some sort. She understood what he'd just done with the little girl. That he'd done it so the others didn't have to. Maybe she forgave him shoving in front of her the entire time.

SA stepped close to Seb as if about to reach out to him, but stopped when Sparks looked up from her computer. "There's no gas leaks on the other side."

A look at the graceful, yellow-skinned woman still a few

metres from him, and Seb sighed at the missed opportunity. He turned to Sparks. The others might not have seen it, but he knew her well enough by now to recognise the relief on her face. None of them liked the thought of an explosion, but it went to the next level with Sparks. It kept her awake at night. He'd shared a room with her. He'd heard her night terrors. "So the third section's sealed off?"

A shrug and Sparks said, "It would seem so. Either that, or there's no gas coming through at all."

As much as Seb wanted to look at SA again, he didn't. The moment had passed and they needed to get on. "That would make our lives a lot easier."

"Which makes me think it's not true," Sparks said. "When has anything gone well for us? Are you all ready?"

"Hang on." Seb walked close to the large double doors, turned his blaster around and drove the butt of it against the steel barrier.

The deep thud boomed through the section they were in and the one beyond.

Bruke whined. "What are you doing?" The green-scaled creature shifted from side to side like he needed to pee.

Seb raised a finger in the air to indicate his friend should wait. And sure enough, the scream came from the other side. Deranged, twisted, and furious, it rushed towards them.

Bruke stepped back from the door moments before a series of thuds clattered into it. Each bang sent him back another pace.

"That's what I'm doing," Seb said with a raised voice so his retreating friend could hear him.

"Trying to get us killed?" Bruke said.

A shake of his head and Seb smiled. "No, I'm trying to flush them out. I'd much rather they were on the other side of that door, waiting for us, than spread throughout this next section and ready to give us a nasty surprise around every damn corner. We can deal with them in one go and be done with it."

Bruke offered another whine in response, but he raised his blaster.

Seb looked at Sparks and then SA. "You both ready?"

As unflappable as ever, SA dipped a nod at Seb, holding him in her gaze for a second. Sparks sighed, shrugged, and said, "Yeah, I suppose so."

CHAPTER 24

Although Sparks stood by the keycard reader with her card in her hand, Seb walked over and flicked his head behind him to indicate where she should go. He gripped his own keycard hanging around his neck as he said, "Get some distance with the others and shoot the zombies when they come through. I should be the one to stay close. Whoever opens this door won't be able to get back to a shooting distance and will have to fight hand to hand. I can do that."

Sparks assessed Seb with her magnified purple gaze, but she didn't argue. Maybe she saw the futility of resisting him. He wouldn't back down on this. He had the skills for close combat. Him and SA, and no way would he expect SA to do it, not after the wasp's nest he'd just kicked.

The screams continued unrelenting on the other side of the doors. They banged against them as if they could beat them down. But no human could punch through the solid barrier, not even Seb with his metal-lined bones.

Seb had intended to get the creatures gathered on the other side of the door, but he'd not been able to comprehend the reality of it until now. He could cope with the rage on the other side, but as soon as he swiped his card through the reader, he'd be setting the mob on his friends.

He hoped they'd given themselves enough space to hold the rush of creatures back. Besides, he'd make sure none of them got through.

A shake ran through Seb's hand when he lifted his card to the reader.

A moment's pause to centre himself and Seb nodded, speaking for the benefit of the others. "Right. Three ... two ... one ..."

Seb swiped the card. He watched the red light turn to green and the crack in the middle of the doors started to open. He backed away a couple of steps and raised his fists as the edges of his world blurred.

The second the flood of zombies appeared, Seb's world slowed down. The monsters swarmed into the space, bringing the reek of rot and waste with them.

SA, Sparks, and Bruke lit the air up with green blasts and knives while Seb waited for the ones they didn't hit to come through.

A widened stance, his fists clenched and raised, Seb had to wait a good few seconds before the first zombie got close enough to him.

A woman, maybe in her thirties, although hard to tell with the haggard expression of rage on her face. Seb punched her square on the nose, driving her back so hard her feet left the ground before she crashed down onto her back.

Shot after shot, knife after knife, the others held the swarm at bay. Despite the width of the narrow gap in the doorway, the zombies had all rushed forward as one, bottlenecking because of their desire to get at the quartet. It slowed them down enough to make them manageable, but the doors were opening wider with every passing second.

Two more broke free and rushed at Seb. Flailing arms and fury came at him. A man and a woman this time. No, he couldn't think of them like that. People with families and lives. Those people had gone. Two monsters. Nothing more.

Seb ducked the swing from the first creature, jumped up, and knocked it back with an uppercut. It fell into the beast behind it and Seb saw a knife fly through the air and sink into the temple of each zombie. It turned them both limp.

A look at SA and Seb nodded his thanks to her. Another scream dragged his attention back to their attackers.

The monsters came in a steady stream at Seb, and although hard work, he managed to keep his pace, dropping them as quickly as they rushed forward.

Fuelled by adrenaline, Seb felt more charged with every punch. Moses might have been a vile creature, but the metal fists were a stroke of genius. He threw another heavy blow into the face of a monster, bones crunching when it fell back as if they'd turned to dust beneath its skin.

The gap in the door grew wider and more zombies flooded out. Where Seb had focused on dropping the ones closest to him, he didn't notice the one who'd circled round and charged at him from his left. The first he knew of it came when it clattered into him, a sharp burn in his ribs as it drove the wind from his lungs.

Seb landed on his back, the creature on top of him. He fought for breath as he stared up at the vile monster and held it at arm's length. Any trace of humanity had been driven from it. It glared at him through red eyes. The castanet click of its teeth snapped just centimetres from him, and it smothered him in a hot halitosis reek.

As Seb looked into the creature's mouth, he momentarily

lost the strength in his arms. Squirming deep in its throat like a lodged piece of food, he saw the tip of a grub as it writhed and twisted. When the zombie snapped its teeth even closer to Seb's face, he yelled and lifted it away from him, his arms shaking beneath the weight of the thing.

CHAPTER 25

Seb pulled at the air with hungry gasps, but he couldn't catch his breath. The zombie had hit him so hard he still hadn't got his wind back. With the weight of the creature on top of him and the pain in his ribs, he started to lose his battle against the beast, his shaking arms giving way beneath its pressure.

Bites snapped closer to Seb's face with the monster's every lurch. The crack of teeth crashing together just missed Seb's nose, all the worse for him seeing it in slow motion. While yelling, he turned his head to the side and continued to push the creature away. He held it at bay but not a lot more.

When the beast screamed again, Seb's arms buckled. He regained control just before the monster fell flat on top of him. Another click of gnashing teeth snapped between them.

A loud whack sounded out and the pressure lifted from Seb. He looked across to see Bruke standing over the thing from where he'd driven the butt of his gun into the side of its face. Bruke then spun his weapon around and shot it.

The blast snapped the zombie rigid for a second and then it fell limp. Seb continued to fight for breath as he stared up at his scaled friend. He dipped a nod at him and Bruke nodded back.

Seb sat up to see all the other creatures had been killed. It had taken no more than about fifteen seconds, although it felt like longer in slow motion. A pile of bodies filled the doorway.

Exhausted from the fight and still trying to catch his breath, Seb smiled at Bruke. "That was close."

Glazed eyes and ragged breaths, Bruke looked on the verge of tears as he glanced between the zombie he'd just killed and Seb. "Are you okay?"

Despite his exhaustion, his arms aching from the strain and build-up of lactic acid, Seb laughed and nodded. "I am. Thank you."

But Bruke didn't look like he could pull himself back. He shook as much as Seb and a tear ran down his face. Although he nodded, he didn't seem to have much else in him.

Once Seb had got to his feet, he looked at the sprawl of bodies on the ground. They formed a considerable mound for them to try to get over. About thirty in total, they all looked dead.

"Well done," Seb said to the others as he walked over to the stinking pile and grabbed the closest corpse. "Although, I think the hardest part is yet to come. We need to stretch these things out in a line so we can take out every grub as they emerge."

The others looked far from pleased with Seb's suggestion, but they didn't argue. And why would they? They'd all seen what happened when the grubs crawled out of their hosts. They all knew they had a few minutes to get better prepared than they were at present.

Where the corridor had been stark whiteness and bleached clean, Seb tarnished it by dragging a line of blood behind the first corpse. A massacre had occurred and the shock red against the white highlighted the fact.

On his trip back to the pile in the doorway, Bruke and SA passed him with their own dead zombies. Sparks didn't help. Too small to be useful at that moment, the others didn't need to discuss it to accept her talents lay elsewhere.

CHAPTER 26

The bodies stretched out in a long line down the corridor. The previous white floor ran slick with their blood. It had coated the bottom of Seb's boots, deep crimson footprints running a trail where he'd walked.

"We need to take a section each," Seb said once he'd counted how many there were. "Forty-two bodies in total." More than he'd initially thought. "You each take ten and I'll take twelve. Make sure you kill enough grubs for the amount of bodies you have."

The middle seemed like the most dangerous place to stand, so Seb took one of the middle sections. SA took the other. Where she'd normally use her knives, she had one of Sparks' blasters again. It made sense to shoot the things. No point in wasting knives on them when they were so close.

Only a few more seconds passed before the first blast. Bruke had done it, and although Seb stood quite far away from him on the other side of SA, he still ruffled his nose against the rotten smell of the dead parasite.

The cheek of a woman by Seb's foot bulged with the strange squirming movement of one of the grubs. No matter how many times he'd witnessed it, he couldn't help but cringe at what looked like reanimation.

Seb shot the woman and the thick reek told him he'd hit the grub.

"Remember to count the parasites," Seb reminded the others. "We need to make sure there's one for every corpse here."

Sparks shot next. Then SA. Bruke fired again. Two, three. Seb ripped off several more shots. Five in total. No idea how many the others had left, he had seven more to go.

CHAPTER 27

"Are we good?" Seb said as he looked up and down the line of dead bodies, the white floor red and glistening with their spilled blood. The now familiar buzz ran through his hands to look at all the corpses. So many lives lost because of the rancid-smelling little grubs. If he needed a motivation to eradicate the disgusting things, it lay on the ground at his feet. Once families, friends, and lovers, they'd now all gone to waste.

When Seb looked to Bruke for his confirmation, the large scaled creature gave him a thumbs-up, but kept his green face staring down at the dead.

A deep sigh and SA nodded.

Sparks had already pulled out her small computer, clearly working out what they had to do next. She nodded while staring at the screen. "Yep."

"Right," Seb said and turned towards the next section of the complex. "Let's go."

Seb entered the next corridor then stopped; it looked similar to the one they'd just come from. Just as illuminated as the last, it stretched away from them and had a set of double doors at the end. Although it ran as long as the previous corridor, it only had three rooms down one side of it.

Before Seb could say anything, Sparks stepped up next to him, her computer still resting on her long palm. She looked down at her screen before pointing at the first room. "That over there's the canteen. That's the sports hall. That's the games room."

Bruke and SA walked up behind Seb and Sparks. Before they got too close, Seb moved off in the direction of the first door—the door to the canteen.

The canteen had a card reader like most other rooms. With a swipe of his card, the red light turned green before the door slid open. When Seb checked the others behind him, SA stepped forwards as if to show she wanted to go in first.

Seb blocked her way. When she scowled and snapped a sharp shrug at him, he said, "Let *me* go in first."

"SA can handle herself," Sparks said.

Another scowl from SA to back up Sparks' comment, but Seb ignored them and walked through the door. There could be something waiting in there, and although she'd deal with it, it could still go wrong. He'd already lost Gurt. He wouldn't let SA go too.

The canteen stretched away from them. Silent and vast, it had the same white floor and walls as the rest of the complex. Rows of white tables ran across the place. Most of the tables had plates on them, some were empty, but many still had stale food on them. The air had the slight funk of decomposition to it. Souring vegetables and gravy. Like a moist compost heap.

"It looks like a ghost ship," Bruke said in a low voice, the hiss of his whisper running away from him.

"I remember hearing rumours about a huge passenger ship called the *Faradis*," Sparks said in an equally quiet voice. "It came close to a space station, but they couldn't get any response when they radioed through. After a few days, they sent a platoon out to board it. It looked like this apparently. As if the crew had just ... vanished."

Bruke gasped, the sound running across the still canteen. He then whispered again, "What happened?"

"I don't know," Sparks said, "but apparently the food was still warm and the coffee still hot."

A chill threatened to twist through Seb, but he shrugged it off. He couldn't get dragged into nonsensical ghost stories. He whispered, "Probably some kind of time/space anomaly."

"That only took the ship's crew?" Sparks said. "And took them a moment before the platoon entered?"

Seb shrugged, and before Sparks could say anything else, he walked to the closest meal. When he pressed his finger against the food, he could feel the group collectively hold their breath. Still keeping his voice low, he hissed, "It's still warm."

Bruke whined and stepped back towards the door. Sparks stared at Seb with wide open eyes. SA still looked pissed off with him. Ghosts didn't scare her.

"And the coffee," Seb whispered while picking up a mug, "is still hot."

A louder whine and Bruke shook his head.

"Bloody hell," Seb said as he looked from Sparks to Bruke, still keeping his voice low. "You two are so gullible. You shouldn't be worrying about ghosts in this place. We know why the canteen looks like this; it's because of those bloody parasites. There's no mystery here."

"That's not funny," Bruke said, his bottom lip poking out.

A wry smile and Seb shrugged. "Not for you maybe." Then before Bruke could start a whispered argument, he added, "The food's cold like it's been this way for several days, maybe longer, which is what we expect, right?"

Bruke dropped his tense shoulders with a hard exhale.

"Come on," Seb said as he turned his back on the group and delved deeper into the canteen.

Even Bruke managed to move quietly as Seb led the way through the place, the butt of his gun pressed into his shoulder while he walked. He'd have taken ghosts over the parasites any day. Ghosts wouldn't bore into his skin and turn him into a madman.

Afraid to blink because the grubs were so hard to spot, Seb's eyes stung as he looked around the room. The infected people weren't the problem. They could see and hear them from a mile away. The grubs, on the other hand, could spring from anywhere.

Because Seb had put so much of his focus on scanning the room, he'd failed to look down. When he stepped on a shard of plate on the floor, the loud crack of breaking porcelain popped through the quiet space like a firecracker.

Seb heard the swift movement behind him of the others raising their weapons. So much for him leading the way and keeping them safe.

Heat spread through Seb's cheeks when he turned to the rest of the crew. The words jammed in his throat, so Seb offered them an apologetic shrug instead. SA continued to scowl at him.

"One good thing about me making that noise," Seb said, his voice louder than before, "is it's shown us it's empty down here."

SA still looked pissed. Since they'd landed on Carstic, Seb had totally disempowered her by taking the lead every single time. But he only did it to protect her. Her scowl deepened like she wanted to cause him physical harm. Then she launched a knife at him.

The blade ran so close to Seb's face he felt the breeze of it against his left cheek.

SA had thrown it so quickly, Seb's world only slipped into slow motion after it had passed him. The whoosh in his ear dragged out because of his slowed perspective finally catching up.

The sound of the blade embedded into bone behind Seb. He turned around as a zombie fell to the ground. It lay on its back, the knife sticking up from the centre of its face.

Heavy breaths and Seb's world sped back up. A look at the downed zombie and back to SA again, and Seb said, "Thank you."

She didn't acknowledge him.

CHAPTER 28

After they'd killed the parasite inside the zombie that nearly got to Seb, they checked the rest of the canteen and the games room. None of them spoke for the entire time and Seb felt SA glaring at him for most of it. But he did his best to ignore her and continued to lead the group. Let her be angry with him. As long as she survived, he'd take her wrath.

When they reached the entrance to the sports hall, Seb didn't even look at SA. He strode in first, Sparks tutting at him as he entered the large space.

The only place in the complex so far—other than the tunnels—not to have a white floor. Soft wood ran the length of the room. It lined the floor as boards butted close enough to one another for there to be no gaps between them. It had various lines in a whole host of colours to mark out different pitches and spaces depending on the game. Basketball rings were attached to the walls. It had a football goal on either side. They even had a climbing wall in one corner. Over in another sectioned-off space, there were skipping ropes, crash mats, and a few other exercise apparatuses.

The air smelled of stale sweat and dust. Seb ruffled his

nose at it. "I suppose it makes sense to have a space like this," he said, his voice echoing through the large arena. "There can't be much else to do down here other than play sports." None of the others replied to him, and when he looked at SA, she turned away.

"At least there's nowhere for the zombies to hide."

"So you don't need SA to save your arse in here, you mean?" Sparks said. "Even though you *still* won't let her go in before you."

Seb shrugged. "I didn't stand on that plate on purpose."

Sparks put her hands on her hips and glared at Seb. She then pointed at SA with one of her long fingers. "In front of you is one of the most badass beings I've ever met. She'd kick your arse in a heartbeat."

Although Seb baulked at the comment, his mind flashed back to how his gift had only kicked in once the knife had passed him. As much as his ego wanted him to fight for it, he had nothing.

"But all you've done since we've been down here is push her back and patronise her. You've been doing it since we landed. You're constraining her at every turn. And then you do things like standing on the plate and put us all in danger."

Seb opened his mouth, but Sparks cut him off.

"And to see how you walked in here. In your haste to be the first in every room, you're getting reckless and putting *all* our lives at risk."

"But ..." Seb looked at SA and back to Sparks.

"You've got to use her for what she does best."

"I don't want her to get hurt." Seb's face flushed hot when he looked at SA. His voice wavered. "I don't want *any* of you to get hurt. I could have helped Gurt on Solsans. I could have healed him. Maybe if I'd stayed back for a few seconds longer. Maybe if I hadn't asked any of you to follow me into battle."

"You didn't ask us," Sparks said.

Bruke then said, "And when Gurt got injured, you *had* to go after Sparks. She would have died on her own in the Countess' palace."

The pain of Gurt's passing ripped at Seb as if a tear ran through the core of his being. Before he could say anything, Bruke added, "You couldn't save them both. You made the choice Gurt wanted you to make. And you believed Gurt would be okay. You had to go after Sparks and the Countess. You had to end her reign."

Seb looked back at SA, the starkness of her bioluminescent gaze boring straight into him. "I can't lose anyone else." He shook to even think about saying it in front of the others, but he kept his focus on her and said it anyway. "Especially you."

The hard frown on SA's face cracked for the briefest moment.

Sparks put a hand on Seb's lower back and spoke with a soft tone. "But can't you see you're driving her away with how you're being? In trying to protect her, you'll make her hate you." She pointed at SA. "That bird should never be caged, Seb, no matter how good your intentions are."

As much as Seb wanted to argue, he didn't have a response. He continued to stare at SA and she continued to stare back. Two steps towards her closed the distance between them. He reached out and lifted her hands up in his. "I'm sorry," he said, a crack in his voice as he thought about Gurt. "I just couldn't live with myself if you died too. I can see I've been an arsehole."

SA's eyebrows rose in the middle and her eyes shifted

from side to side as she looked into one of his eyes and then the other.

"You think we don't all feel the pain of losing Gurt?" Sparks then said. "We're all struggling with it, but no one blames you, Seb."

"But you came back to fight beside me. To join in a war *I* started."

"We came back because you were fighting for a good cause. We wanted to fight for it too. You need to stop blaming yourself. We all made our own choice. We're all adults."

Seb still hadn't let go of SA's hands, and when he looked at her, she nodded along with Sparks. "Can we start again?" he said. "I'll try to stop crushing you. Although that was never my intention, I can see now how it must make you feel. I don't think you're weak. Sparks is right, you'd kick my arse."

A broad smile spread across SA's face and she covered her mouth as if to stifle a laugh.

"And you've saved me on more than one occasion. I never meant to disrespect you. My intentions have always been true, even if my actions are a little misguided." The words kept coming, running away with Seb as he said, "I just wanted to—"

But before Seb could say anything else, SA leaned forwards and kissed him on the cheek.

So close he felt her body heat, Seb's head spun and his heart raced. Any words that had been in his mind before then vanished and his breathing quickened.

It took for Sparks to say, "Come on," as she left the sports hall—the others following her—before Seb moved again. This time he let the others lead the way to the double doors between them and the mining section.

CHAPTER 29

Seb rode the high of SA's kiss out of the gym. For the first time since they'd landed on Carstic, he let go of his need to control. The others were adults and could look after themselves. The warmth of SA's lips still remained against his cheek. How long would he have to wait before she did it again?

The same white glare Seb had got used to hit him when he stepped out of the dusty gym into the stark corridor. The smell of sweat and dust gave way to the disinfectant reek of bleach tinged with rot.

Sparks led the way, SA and Bruke walking side by side behind her. For the first time since they'd been down there, Seb held back.

By the keycard reader with her mini-computer in her hand, Sparks looked at the screen as she said, "I'd suggest leaving your blasters here. There are strong traces of ruthane on the other side of this door. It's safe to breathe, but a laser blast will set the place off like an atomic bomb. Oh, and SA, you might want to leave your knives too. A spark from one of them could also ignite the air."

Although SA put her gun she'd borrowed from Sparks down, she kept her knives strapped to her. She pulled out two and held one in each hand. As if to reassure Sparks she could use them responsibly, she gripped them hard and held them up to her.

"As long as you don't throw them," Sparks said.

SA nodded her compliance.

After SA and Bruke stepped away from placing their weapons by the door, Seb walked over and put his semi-automatic down. When he turned around, he made eye contact with SA, who smiled at him. Heat rushed through his cheeks and he smiled back.

While Seb stood there, grinning like an idiot, he nearly didn't see it. The slightest of movements, something dropped from the ceiling in his peripheral vision. His world slipped into slow motion and he turned to see the grub land on Sparks' arm. Before he could react, the thing had burrowed its fat head through her sleeve.

Too late to stop it, Seb shouted, "No!" and rushed to his friend.

Although he grabbed her right arm and lifted it, the grub had already vanished from sight. It left a stain of blood on her shirt.

Seb dug his fingers into the hole on Sparks' sleeve and tore it wider. The space where the grub had just burrowed into had healed up already. Had he imagined it? But his hands buzzed with the need to heal her. "What the?"

A look at the others and Seb said, "Did you guys see that?" He spun back to Sparks before giving them a chance to respond. "Did a grub just dig into you?"

But Sparks didn't reply. Instead, she stared at Seb with a blank gaze.

"Sparks?"

Before Seb could say anything else, a convulsion snapped through Sparks and her eyes rolled back in her head.

The echo of Seb's voice ran away from him up the empty corridor, his desperation thrown back at him several-fold. "*Sparks?!*"

CHAPTER 30

Another several convulsions followed straight on the heels of the first as Sparks fitted in Seb's grip. He had a hold of the tops of both of her arms, his shoulders and pecs locked tight as he tried to keep her still. But it seemed pointless, restraining her wouldn't stop the parasite from taking her over.

White splutters of foam stuttered from Sparks' mouth, and the purple eyes Seb knew so well had rolled back in her head. He only saw the whites of her eyeballs.

Then they snapped back, the purple irises gone as Sparks fixed Seb with the same red glare he now associated with the zombies. They'd lost her. His stomach sank and a lump clawed at his throat. But he wouldn't give up on her. No way.

As Seb stared into his friend's small face—her blood-red glare magnified behind her glasses—his breaths ran away with him. "This isn't going to happen to you, Sparks."

She might have only been tiny, but when Sparks raised her top lip in a snarl and glared rage at Seb, he jolted backwards from the shock of it. For a moment, he almost let go of her.

Seb quickly regained his senses, and in one fluid movement, he slipped around behind her, gripped her with one arm across her small chest, and used his free hand to hold the spot on her right arm where the grub had burrowed into.

Since their trip to Solsans, Seb's hands had buzzed whenever he got close to a wounded being. Even corpses triggered his desire to heal them. But now, with his grip over the space where the grub had burrowed into Sparks, he felt nothing. The buzzing desire to heal her only moments ago must have come from where the creature had entered her. But that had fully healed now.

"Come on," Seb shouted as Sparks twisted and writhed against his restraint.

Growls and snarls, Sparks angled her face in Seb's direction and bit at the air separating them. Desperate to attack him, she twisted and writhed to try to get free of his tight hold.

Not knowing what else to do, Seb kept his hand over the spot where the grub had entered her body, but still no buzz ran through his hand. "You can beat this, Sparks." A blurred vision from his tears and he shouted so loud his voice broke. "Not again. This isn't going to happen again. No way."

Both SA and Bruke watched Seb. He opened his mouth to shout at them to do something, but what could they do? What could any of them do? Before he could say anything else, SA turned and ran back into the sports hall they'd just emerged from.

CHAPTER 31

SA returned from the gym with one of the skipping ropes in her hands.

"What are you doing?" Seb said to her. Not that he'd get an answer.

When she got close enough, she made a motion to show him she wanted to tie Sparks up.

"And then what?" Seb said, his pulse racing as he tried to hold onto his rage. "What can we do with her then?"

"She'll be easier for us to take with us that way," Bruke said.

Seb scowled at the green beast. "What do you know?"

Bruke stepped back a couple of paces as if Seb's words had dealt him a physical blow. He pressed his hand against his chest, clearly hurt by Seb's attack.

Seb's pulse raced and he gritted his teeth. "Acting like that isn't going to help. It's about time you grew a spine." The edges of his vision blurred as his gift threatened to kick in.

SA reached over and put a hand on Seb's shoulder. The serene bioluminescent gaze calmed him a little, and when he felt Sparks fight harder than before to get at SA, he let go of some of the tension in his body. They had to restrain her so she didn't harm them.

A heavy sigh and Seb nodded. "You're right. I'm sorry, Bruke."

Not one to hold a grudge, the apology seemed to be enough for Bruke, who stepped forward and said, "Let me hold her while SA ties her up."

Seb waited for Bruke to take Sparks. He then stepped away, watching the other two tie her arms to her sides with the skipping rope.

"I'm going to find a way to help her," Seb said as he took in his bound little friend. "Even if it means taking her back with us to Aloo. I'll fight Moses to make sure she gets the best medical care. I'm going to find a way to fix her."

The other two didn't reply. Seb saw in their concerned frowns that they wanted to help her as much as he did.

CHAPTER 32

Seb wanted to abort the mission there and then. Sparks had now become his number one priority. But Moses wouldn't pick them up if they didn't eradicate the parasites from the mines. And they couldn't fly out of there now their pilot had been compromised.

A look at the still-sealed doors to the mine, Seb said, "We need to get this section cleared as quickly as possible so we can get the hell out of here." Bruke had stepped several paces back with Sparks in his arms. "Are you sure you're okay holding her?"

"With no weapons allowed beyond those doors—" Bruke grimaced as he fought against the fitting Sparks "—I've got nothing else to offer. I'm best suited to keeping her restrained."

Not strictly true, but he certainly had less to offer than the other two. It made sense for Bruke to keep a hold of Sparks. Between Seb and SA, they could face whatever came their way.

"Okay," Seb said and walked up to the closed doors separating them from the mines. He drove a hard punch against them, the *boom* of his blow calling out into the area beyond.

The group hadn't exactly been quiet up until that point, but the sound seemed to stir up the zombies on the other side. It took just a few seconds for their screams to light up the air and for the stampeding rush of footsteps to come towards them.

An increased heart rate from the sound, Seb jumped when the first thud crashed against the other side of the doors. Several more bodies slammed against the doors after it.

Seb moved over to the card reader and looked at SA. "I'll open the door and then join you in the fight, yeah?"

The same calm look she always wore, SA raised her knives to show she was ready.

Just before he could swipe his card through the reader, Seb heard Sparks making more noise than before. When he looked at her, she seemed even more agitated than previously, spittle flying from her mouth as she twisted and shook in Bruke's grip.

SA looked back at her too.

Seb frowned at her behaviour before he said, "It's like—"

"She can sense the zombies on the other side," Bruke finished for him.

"Yeah." The sound on the other side of the door picked up, so the yells and screams rang even louder. "And they can sense her."

A deep breath to settle himself and Seb looked at SA again. "I'm not sure that tells us anything we didn't already know. The zombies aren't exactly quiet, so it's not like we need an early warning. You ready?"

SA nodded, so Seb ran his card through the reader. The red light on the screen turned green.

CHAPTER 33

The stench of ruthane, or rather, the flatulent reek of the additive mixed with the gas, rushed forward with the wave of zombies.

They ran straight at SA, who looked as calm as ever. A tight grip on her blades, she dropped down into a defensive crouch. Being the first thing the creatures were faced with, every one of them headed for her.

It gave Seb the opportunity to surprise them. He ran from the side, his world slowing down as he got close to the first one. But he stopped short of the pack.

It had been hard enough to kill the zombies before. Especially when he'd seen the lives they'd lived; connected with them as human beings. But now, with Sparks as one of them, he froze. They were the victims in all of this. They deserved saving like he planned to save Sparks.

A woman then jumped at Seb and he caught sight of her attack in his peripheral vision. Too slow to react, he noticed the woman's mouth stretch wide as she readied to bite him.

Moments before she sank her teeth into him, a glint of a blade flashed through the air and embedded in the side of her face. Without SA, he would be dead ten times over by now. The fight left the woman as she turned limp mid-flight and crashed at Seb's feet.

Seb looked at SA. She'd already pulled out a new blade and continued fighting the majority of the crowd. She had them beat by the look of things.

It helped snap Seb out of it. He couldn't save them all. He swung for the next zombie close to him. The crunch of bone responded to his catching her clean on the temple. Her legs folded beneath her and she turned limp like many of the others.

Every blow hurt Seb's heart. But they needed taking down. If he had any chance of getting Sparks and the others off Carstic, the creatures in front of them needed to be gone.

Besides, the zombies looked tormented. Twisted masks of suffering, Seb punched another one square in the face, dropping it with one blow like he had most of them. And he couldn't take them all back to the Shadow Order's base. Hell, he'd have a fight just getting Sparks back there.

By the time Seb had dropped three or four of the creatures, SA had taken out twice that amount and she didn't look like slowing down any time soon.

Seb saw his own remorse in SA's expression, but they were doing what they had to. These things needed to be stopped. He punched the next creature to come near him.

CHAPTER 34

"Only fifteen this time," Seb said as they stood over the bodies of the fallen. They'd killed every grub to come from their mouths and the air reeked of ruthane and rot.

"Although, I suppose it makes sense," Seb said. "There would be more of them in the communal areas because there would have been more hosts there. Hopefully we've got them all now."

A cocked eyebrow from SA made Seb nod. "You're right, we can't expect it to be free of zombies down there. And the grubs have to be coming from somewhere too, I suppose."

Seb looked at Bruke and then Sparks. She'd calmed down a little. Now all the grubs had been killed, she seemed far less agitated. The same twist of fury might have distorted her features, but it looked muted compared to what he'd witnessed only moments before.

A nervous Bruke said, "I reckon she'll give us an early warning when the grubs or zombies are near."

Not surprising, he felt nervous about that; the mines could have hundreds of the little worms in them still. They didn't choose for Sparks to be in her current state, but they might as well make the most of it. If she served as an early warning system, they should use it. They needed all the help they could get. Hard not to be facetious, Seb finally said, "Every cloud and that."

The mine section of the complex looked much more like the tunnel they'd entered through. It had exposed rock on the walls rather than soil. The ground looked to be as infirm and soggy. Wires ran every which way from where they hadn't bothered to conceal them. Poor lighting from solitary bulbs hung from the ceiling.

"This should be fun," Seb said as he stared ahead, his voice running down the tunnel away from them.

Silence from Bruke and SA. Although, what did he expect?

"Right," Seb said, his stomach twisting tighter to look into the gloom. "We need to get this done. Get this place cleared out. Bruke, watch Sparks for any sign of a reaction. We need to get down there, clear the grubs and zombies out, and get back to Aloo. Does anyone have anything else to add?"

A look at SA and her deep frown and Seb laughed. "Sounds like a simple plan, doesn't it?"

Although SA continued to look at him, her expression remained unchanged.

Before they moved off, Seb said, "Oh, one more thing." He walked up to Sparks and fished the radio from her top pocket. She snarled and snapped, biting at the space between her and his hand. But Bruke restrained her well enough to prevent her from being a threat.

Once he'd freed the radio, Seb pressed the button on the side of it. It hissed before connecting with the shuttle that had brought them in. "This is Seb. We're going to need someone to pick us up in about thirty minutes."

"Why can't you fly out?"

"Our pilot ..." Seb paused for a moment before he said, "She's hurt. She can't possibly fly."

Static hissed from the radio's speaker for a few seconds and Seb looked at both Bruke and SA. They watched the radio, waiting like him.

"Okay," the voice finally came through, "see you up top in thirty minutes."

"Thank you, over and out."

Despite the vicious Sparks doing everything she could to get at him again, Seb slipped the radio back into her top pocket. Like she'd done only moments previously, she bit and thrashed in her desperation to make any kind of contact with him.

"SA," Seb said, "you move much more quietly than I do. Can you lead the way?"

Of course she saw Seb's request as a way to make up for being a douche, but SA nodded all the same and walked with her usual grace into the third and final section of the mining complex. Seb followed her with Bruke and Sparks close behind.

They'd walked no more than five or six paces before Sparks grew more agitated again.

SA stopped and looked back at her.

The small Thrystian's red eyes had widened and she bit at the air. She twisted and turned, growled and spat.

However, when Seb looked down into the darkness, he couldn't see anything. He couldn't hear anything either. The usual stampede didn't come at them. "Maybe she's not an early warning system."

Before Bruke could reply, Seb saw it. One at first, it

moved over land as a small fat projectile. His world slowed down again just as he said, "Grubs."

Before the first one had reached them, a wave of them rolled from the darkness behind it. Seb fought against his rising panic and muttered, "Shit!"

CHAPTER 35

Seb had no blasters now they'd entered the next section, and SA couldn't risk throwing her knives. They waited for the onrushing grubs to come to them. There looked to be an impossible amount and it took all he had not to turn tail and run.

When the first one got close enough, Seb stamped down hard. The creature's fat little body gave the slightest resistance before it popped like a sauce sachet.

Several more came at them and it took all Seb had to keep his head.

At first they came forward in ones and twos, but soon more and more rushed behind them. Every stamp on the hard ground ran up Seb's legs and stung his knees, but he crushed five, six, seven of the grotesque things at a time.

One landed on Seb's shin. A quick bat with his hand and he knocked it away. It left a hole in the fabric of his trousers. To look at it damn near paralysed him. So close to becoming a zombie. But he didn't have time to think about it. He stamped on several more of the gross little bugs.

The reek of rot hung heavier than ever. The floor glistened with their spilled essence. At least one hundred grubs down already, the pack didn't show any sign of thinning.

All the while, Seb listened to Sparks fitting behind them. She snarled and growled, riled up by the presence of so many of the parasites. He wanted to go to his friend and calm her down. But the only thing that would do that would be the complete eradication of the grubs. Then he could comfort her all he wanted.

Even when stamping on the parasites, SA moved with grace. A frantic dance, she squashed them in groups. She coped better than Seb. He'd been a fool to think he could protect her.

Another grub landed on Seb. This time on his arm while he'd been watching SA. He looked down to see the back end of it vanish inside his shirt.

CHAPTER 36

Were it not for his world moving in slow motion, then Seb would have gone the way of Sparks. The very slightest sting of the grub bit into his flesh. He wedged his fingers in the hole in his shirt, gripped the back of its fat little body, and halted its potentially deadly progress.

Squishy in his grip, Seb dragged the creature out. It writhed and twisted, snapping from side to side. He threw it back down the tunnel with the others and returned to stamping them out.

They'd agreed it would have been better for SA not to use her knives, but as the rush of grubs thinned a little, she launched one behind them in the direction of Sparks and Bruke.

The blade glinted in the poor light as it flew straight through the thick body of one of the grubs. It cut the thing in two, dropping it before it could reach Bruke.

The knife continued to fly at the rocky wall and Seb's shoulders wound tight. It hit it. Thankfully it didn't make a spark. A relieved sigh and he looked back at the ever-calm

SA. They should have trusted she could use her knives appropriately in the highly explosive mine. The blades were an extension of her and she knew them intimately.

CHAPTER 37

Bruke had been correct to point out how much Sparks helped them in her current state. To look at her calmer, but still furious face made Seb nod. "I think that's all of them. There may be more farther down, but I think we're good for the immediate area."

The floor ran slick with the clear liquid that filled the grubs. The smell of rot hung so heavy, Seb heaved several times, lifting the acidic burn of bile on the back of his throat.

After a look at SA, Seb nodded and said, "You were amazing. Let's hope this is nearly over."

SA nodded back, and together they led the way farther down the dank tunnel into the mines.

CHAPTER 38

Other than Sparks, the group moved deeper into the mines in near silence. The smell of the grubs' spilled essence gave way to a muggy damp reek of wet earth. It smelled stronger than even the agent added to the ruthane.

The soft ground underfoot muted their steps, but the sound of their march still called ahead into the tunnel. Probably a good thing to let the grubs know they were coming. If their behaviour so far had been anything to go on, they rushed at their prey with little regard for stealth. The more noise the quartet made, the more of the horrible little worms they could flush out of hiding.

Seb listened to Bruke's heavy breaths as he fought against Sparks' struggle. Sparks offered her own growling, snarling protest. She sounded like an animal possessed. And, in a way, she was.

On the plus side, she sounded much better than she had done when the zombies and the grubs were nearby. Sure, it hurt Seb's heart to hear his friend in her current state. But they would find a way to help her—they had to—and at that moment, hearing her calmer was the only comfort he could find.

Just as the thought left Seb's mind, Sparks growled behind him and his entire frame slumped. "Great," he said, his voice calling down into the gloom ahead of them before he turned back to look at his thrashing friend. To see her increased fury made him sigh. "Just great."

Several blinks did little to appease the itch in Seb's tired eyes. He couldn't see any better into the gloom either. No doubt something would rush them at any moment. The edges of his world blurred and he clenched his fists, his arms aching from the previous battles, his legs leaden as he stopped moving and waited for the next rush of whatever would come their way.

CHAPTER 39

But nothing came.
They waited for a few minutes, staring into the dark and at one another, hunched down and ready to fight, but nothing came.

When SA moved next to Seb, he looked across at her. She walked over to a wall close to them, and he suddenly saw it too. It had been hidden in the poor light, but now he'd seen it, it seemed so obvious.

A pile of fallen rocks—freshly fallen by the look of things—covered what seemed to be the entrance to a cave or alcove of some sort. Seb walked over to it and he listened to Bruke and Sparks follow behind them. The closer they got, the more agitated Sparks became. She spat and hissed, the sound of struggle from where Bruke tried to clearly hold her back.

"Whatever's in there," Seb said, "I doubt we're going to be pleased to see it." His pulse quickened as he stared at it. "But we can't leave it. We've been sent down here with a mission to clear out this entire colony. I couldn't care less whether Moses gets paid or not, but I won't be able to live with myself if another community gets sent down here and they get wiped out too. We have to clear this place."

A look at SA and she waited. Sometimes, it seemed, he should lead. Seb reached forward and pulled one of the small rocks away from the pile. It revealed a hole no larger than the width of one of the fat grubs.

Tentative at first, Seb leaned towards the hole, his heart pounding as he pushed his face closer, but not too close. He couldn't give the grubs that opportunity. What better way into his system than through his eyeball?

Behind him, Sparks seemed more agitated. If only she could tell them what she knew.

As much as Seb wanted to peer through the hole, his curiosity could kill him. He turned to SA, pointed at it, and said, "What if there are grubs in there?"

SA nodded at the larger boulders blocking the way.

"Move one of them?" Seb said.

SA nodded, raised her knives, and hunched down to show she'd fight if she needed to.

It made sense to throw the space open wide rather than put his face too close.

When Seb reached down and grabbed one of the large rocks, the voice of what sounded like a young girl came from the other side. "Please," it said, "leave us alone."

The sound forced Seb back several paces and he looked at SA. She stared back for a second before they both turned to look at the fallen rocks again.

CHAPTER 40

"We're here to help," Seb said to the hole in the rocks.

This time, a man's voice spoke, catching Seb off guard. "How do we know that? How do we know you're not one of *them*?"

A shrug, and Seb half-laughed when he said, "Because we're not snarling and hissing."

The man paused long enough for Seb to listen to Sparks behind him. "Okay, *she* is, but we have her restrained."

"Why do you have one of them with you?"

"She's our friend."

"Half the people in these mines are our friends."

"But we have just one. It's easy to restrain one. Especially as she's not even four feet tall."

Impatience rode the man's words. "What do you want?"

"We've been sent down here to clear the place of the parasites. To make it habitable again."

"By who?"

"The Shadow Order."

"*Who?*"

"Look"—Seb shook his head to himself—"it doesn't matter if you've heard of them or not, more that you understand why we're here. We're here to help. So let us help you."

"We're okay, thanks. We're doing fine as we are."

"I hate to break this to you, but you're trapped in a small alcove in a dingy mine with potentially more horrible parasites waiting to attack you."

The man didn't reply.

"I'm guessing you're a little low on resources in there?"

The man still didn't respond.

"We're going to move these rocks away."

Yet more silence.

Seb grabbed the boulder in front of him, but the huge cold rock didn't budge. As high as it was wide, the top of it stood about a foot taller than Seb.

SA joined Seb and tugged on the rocks, but they still didn't shift, not even an inch.

"Stand back," Seb said to the people on the other side, his call running away from him down into the dark mines. A deep breath to slow the world down and he saw the boulder's weakest spot. Fortunately, it sat right on the front of it. He balled his metal fist and drove a hard blow into it.

The rock shattered under the impact of Seb's punch, turning into a thousand small shards. The other boulders resting on top of it all fell forward and he had to jump back so his feet didn't get crushed.

Closer to Sparks now, he heard her agitation ring louder than before.

It took a few seconds for the dust to clear, but when it did, Seb saw the man he'd spoken to. He looked to be in his midforties. He carried a bit too much weight for his five-foot-nine to five-foot-ten-inch frame. Black hair and a round face.

Although all of the details fell from Seb's mind when he looked at the blaster the man had trained on him.

"You know if you use that, it'll blow this entire place up, right?" Seb said.

The man still didn't speak.

What must have been the man's family cowered behind him in the cave. A small skinny blonde girl of no more than about ten years old, and a woman about the same age as the man. It might have been his wife. They looked tired, dirty, and hungry.

At first, Seb didn't see it in the poor light, but then he noticed they all had cracked and dry lips. "You look like you need some water. How long have you been in here for?"

The man didn't answer. Instead, he raised his gun and jabbed it in Seb's direction. "I'm not afraid to use this."

"I'm sure, but you haven't used it yet, so I'm guessing you don't want to if you can avoid it."

Sweat beaded the man's brow and he looked at his wife before returning his attention to Seb. "Get out of my way." His blaster shook at the end of his outstretched arm. "Blowing us all up has to be better than whatever you lot have planned for me."

A look at SA and then Bruke, Seb turned back to the man and shrugged. "What do we have planned for you?"

"You look like bad people. I mean, look at you."

"Wow," Seb said. "What a way to thank someone."

SA placed a hand on her hip while she stared at the man and cocked her head to the side.

But the man didn't respond, a mixture of anger, shame, and fear twisting through his chubby face.

Seb looked at SA and shrugged. "If he wants to go, we should let him. I'm sure his escape plan from this wretched planet is much better than ours. Who wants a lift out of here when you can walk through the radiation desert up there?" Together, they stepped aside to let the man through, revealing Sparks in her fitting, convulsing, and furious state.

Only small, but occupied with a vicious rage, Sparks continued to snap at the air as if trying to get to the three people. More beings around her—especially humans, it would seem—had clearly stirred her up. Although the fact she felt calmer around the other Shadow Order members suggested she had some recollection of who they were, that some small part of Sparks remained in the monster Seb saw when he looked at her.

The man with the gun led the way and the woman followed behind him. She helped the little girl, who had a crude splint on her leg. Seb hadn't noticed it until that moment. Probably because he had a gun in his face. Now he looked at the splint, he saw a few long shards of rock had been used to hold her leg in place. They'd been bound to her with what looked to be an old coat.

When the man with the gun drew level with Sparks, he moved too quickly for Seb or SA to react, catching them off guard as he raised his weapon and pointed it at her face. "I'm sorry," he said, his voice getting louder with his clear panic, "but I can't let this monstrosity live. I've seen an entire complex wiped out by these things. They *have* to be eradicated."

CHAPTER 41

SA reacted before Seb could. A flash of movement, she exploded to life and rugby tackled the man around his waist.

Slower than SA again, Seb's world slipped into slow motion as he watched the podgy man take the impact like he'd been hit by a train.

They slammed down on the hard ground, the man's chubby body bearing most of the blow. He let out a bark-like, "*Oomph*."

Before the man could do anything else, SA had taken his blaster from his hand and slid it across the ground to Seb. He picked it up and put it in his pocket.

Although Seb watched SA and the man, he noticed the woman drag the small girl back into the cave they'd emerged from. A raised hand to halt them, he said, "We're here to help. *Please* trust me when I say we really don't want to hurt you. As long as you don't try to harm us, you have nothing to worry about."

A look down at the podgy man and Seb watched him writhe and twist beneath SA, who currently sat on him. "I'd give that up if I were you. Ten times out of ten she'd kick your arse, so you might as well save your energy."

Although he regarded Seb with a hard scowl, the man fell slightly limp beneath SA's pressure as if he'd taken the advice.

When Seb looked at the woman and the girl, he saw they hadn't pulled any farther away, so he walked over to the man and crouched down next to him. Soft words, he said, "We don't want to harm you. You need to trust that."

The man looked up at Sparks, his eyes wide in his red face. He continued to stare at her while he spoke. "It's not *you* I'm worried about."

"Yeah, well, you just have to accept her. We'll keep her away from you and your family. Look at her, she won't get out of those bonds any time soon. And even if she does, have you seen the size of Bruke's arms? She isn't going anywhere. Now tell me, what's happened to the girl. Is she your daughter?"

"Yes. She's called Hannah, and my wife is Alison. My name's Wilson."

"What happened to Hannah's leg?"

"A boulder fell on it. I think it's broken."

Just the thought of it sent Seb's hands tingling. He could finally put them to use. "Okay, Wilson, you stay there and I'm going to help Hannah, okay?"

Another shake as if he could buck SA from him and Wilson's voice rose in pitch. "What are you going to do?"

"I'm going to help her. Not that you have any choice in your current predicament, but you need to trust me."

The man stared at Seb but didn't respond. The expression on his face showed his acceptance of what he couldn't change, but he looked a long way from trusting him.

Seb walked over to the girl, his hands buzzing so hard he expected them to hum.

Frozen to the spot, Alison stared at Seb, the same mistrust on her face as her husband's.

When Seb dropped down next to them and put his hands on Hannah's leg, Wilson shouted at him, "What the *hell* are you doing to my daughter?"

But Seb didn't answer. Instead, he felt the buzz in his hands and breathed through it as he visualised the bone in Hannah's leg knitting back together.

A deep warmth ran through Seb's hands, and when he looked up at Hannah, he saw the relief on her withdrawn face as he took her pain away. Although the small child trembled at his touch, he could see her slowly relax and trust him much quicker than either of her parents had.

After just a few seconds, Seb pulled away from her and smiled. "Better?"

Hannah smiled back and Seb saw Alison relax a little at her response. A firm nod and the girl said, "Yes." After she'd looked at her mum and dad, she looked back at Seb. "Much better. Thank you."

"You're like them," Wilson said, awe and fear in his tone as he sat up, SA having moved away from him.

"Like who?"

"The grubs."

"*What?* I'm nothing like them!"

A shake of his head and Wilson raised his hands defensively. "No, sorry, I didn't mean that how it sounded. You can heal wounds like them. I'd never seen any being with an ability to heal until I saw them."

A look at Sparks, and although Seb couldn't see the spot that had healed after the grub had gone in, he remembered it. "I've seen it too. So they all heal the wounds they've made?"

"That's my experience," Wilson said.

"Almost as if—"

"They want to preserve their host for as long as possible," Wilson finished for him.

Seb stood up from his crouch beside Hannah's leg, walked over to Wilson, and reached down to help him get to his feet. "Let's start again. I'm Seb; this is SA, Bruke, and Sparks. We're from the Shadow Order and we're here to help you."

Although he looked at Sparks like he expected her to attack him—and he should feel that way because she certainly wanted to—Wilson let Seb help him up and said, "Thank you. I'm sorry I got spooked."

"It's understandable, she wants to bite your face off."

Wilson looked at Sparks again.

"Now tell us," Seb said. "How did you end up here?"

CHAPTER 42

"We were eating in the canteen with most of the community at the time," Wilson said. "It was dinner, and you could always guarantee that at least eighty percent of us would be there."

"And the others?" Seb asked.

"Working. This place ran all day and night. A licence to print credits, the Camorons wouldn't have a moment where the mine wasn't capturing ruthane." After a pause as if managing the trauma of what they'd been through, he said, "We were lucky to be close to the door when everything kicked off. It gave us the chance to run."

"So why run into the mines?"

"The insanity was kicking off the other way. The grubs came in from outside."

Seb nodded.

Wilson pointed at a sledgehammer resting against the wall in the alcove. "On our way down, we picked that up. I knew about the small cave, and with a dead end down that way"—he pointed down the tunnel—"it seemed like the best place to hide."

"And cave in the entrance so nothing could get to you?" Seb said.

"I didn't know what else to do."

"And that's how Hannah got hurt?"

Wilson let go of a deep sigh and dropped his attention to the ground. "Yep. A rock landed on her leg. I should have been more careful."

When Seb looked at Hannah, he saw Alison stand up from where she'd removed the splint from her daughter's leg. The girl smiled as she swayed from side to side, testing out her ability to stand. "Don't be too hard on yourself. If it wasn't for your quick thinking, your family would be dead. We've not found any other survivors down here."

A sad twist ran through Wilson's features. "I worried I'd crippled her for life." He looked up at Seb, a glaze of tears covering his eyes. "Thank you so much for helping her. And thank you for helping us out of here. Another day or so and we would have died of thirst."

Seb looked at the deep red cracks in Wilson's lips. A white tinge of dry skin ran across them.

"Although," Wilson said, "I would have rather died of thirst than get taken over by those *things*." A gasp and his eyes spread wide. He looked at Sparks. "I'm sorry, I didn't mean to say that. I—"

But Seb waved the comment away. "We'll get you all out of here. We just need to clear this section and then we're ready to go."

"Do you have any water?" Wilson asked.

Seb shook his head. "Sorry."

After he'd looked at Sparks again, the vicious little creature spitting and hissing at him, Wilson turned back to Seb. "Tell me if I'm being out of line, but *why* are you keeping her alive?"

"I can't kill her," Seb said. "Not until we've taken her to our base and have them try everything they can to bring her back." The memory of Gurt threw him off and a lump rose in his throat. After he'd cleared it, he added, "We've been through a lot together and I can't give up on her."

"You would if you'd seen what we have."

Seb shook his head. "No, I wouldn't. We've just fought against them and have first-hand experience of what those creatures are like. It's different when there's just one though, eh? Especially one so small and easy to restrain. A complex full of them and there's nothing for it but to kill them."

"Not necessarily," Wilson said.

"Huh?"

"I have a theory. I've had a lot of time to think over the past few days and I think I know how to help the people with parasites in them."

"Go on."

"These creatures behave like they're of one mind, right? Hunting as one, driving their hosts to kill as one."

"Right."

"Some creatures with the same mentality have a queen. Something driving their hive mind."

"So the zombies have a queen?"

"Zombies?"

"Humour me," Seb said. "So if they *do* have a queen, and if we kill it, then we'll get Sparks back?"

"I think so, yes."

Seb looked at SA and Bruke as he replied to Wilson. "Well, we need to take the grubs down anyway, so we'll make sure we find the queen and kill her."

"Now, it's just a theory."

"But you're confident it will work?"

"I'd bet on it if I was a betting man, but confident? No."

Hope lifted through Seb's heart. "It's as good a plan as any. And it's what we have to do anyway. Let's go and find the queen."

"It shouldn't be hard to find her," Wilson said.

"Oh?"

"Although they came in from the hangar, I think they'll hide their queen as far from the complex's entrance as they can to keep her safe."

Another look at SA and Bruke, Seb then said, "Okay, we have to go down into the mines anyway. You'll be safer with us than without, so let's do this."

CHAPTER 43

SA led the way, walking a few metres ahead of Seb and Wilson. Behind them walked Wilson, Alison, and their child, Hannah. Bruke kept Sparks a safe distance even farther back.

Because he had SA's eyes up ahead and the early warning system Sparks had become, Seb didn't quite relax, but felt comfortable that he'd get at least a slight heads-up on the next attack.

Although, when Seb looked back at Sparks as she shook and spat in her clear desire to get at Wilson and his family, he tensed up again. Maybe the presence of the other humans would make her alarm ineffective. SA would notice any problems up ahead though, and surely the grubs would have made their presence known if they'd passed or approached them up until that point. Whatever threat remained in the mines, it had to be farther down the dark tunnel.

After another wary look back at Sparks, Wilson turned to Seb and said, "So why do you have a Thrystian with you? They're a typically antisocial and ruthless race."

"Oh, she's ruthless all right," Seb said. "But she's probably quite different from your average Thrystian. She got away from her home world as soon as she could. She hated the place."

After he'd looked at Sparks again, staring at her as if she could slip her bonds and attack his family, Wilson returned his attention to the dark tunnel in front of them.

"Let me ask you something," Seb said to the man. "If you had this theory about the queen and what killing her would do, why did you try to kill Sparks? I mean, you think she can be saved, right?"

More vehement than ever, almost as if she'd heard Seb's question, Sparks shook and twisted as she fought to get at Wilson's family.

"Because of that," Wilson said. "I have a wife and daughter I need to protect. It's nothing personal against ... Sparks? Is that her name?"

Seb nodded.

"Just more that I want to make sure my family doesn't get hurt. That's always going to be more important to me than the life of a stranger."

Another nod and Seb looked down the tunnel again. SA still seemed on top of things.

The farther they went into the mine, the darker it got. They'd had the bright shine from the open doors leading to the recreational area behind them, but they were now stepping out of its reach. Had they not loaded the doors with dead bodies, making it impossible for them to close, they wouldn't have even had that.

"And a shantarac," Wilson said.

"Huh?" Seb said, ruffling his nose as a particularly strong hit of ruthane smothered him.

"Your green scaly friend is from a planet called Raunce. He's a shantarac. They're a peaceful race, but if you provoke them, they flip into a berserker rage. It takes a lot, but when they go, you'd best get out of their way."

Seb looked from Bruke back to Wilson.

"Have you seen him lose it?" Wilson said.

Seb couldn't help but smile. "Yeah."

A widening of his eyes and Wilson's entire flabby face lit up. "Quite impressive, isn't it?"

After he'd watched Wilson for a few seconds, Seb nodded. "It really is. Although it takes a lot to get Bruke to that point." He then checked SA again.

"And the scarpist," Wilson said.

When Seb saw him looking at SA, he said, "What do you know about her?" Maybe he sounded too keen.

"Not much. They're a very agile race that comes from the planet Delvin. Most of them are deadly and graceful. They have a calm temperament, almost zen-like."

As Wilson described SA, Seb continued to watch her. Her body moved like a cat's, graceful and almost silent as she travelled down the tunnel on high alert. "They're amazing, aren't they?"

When Wilson didn't reply, Seb looked across to see the man smiling at him. "Anyway," Seb said, heat rushing through his cheeks, "how do you know all this?"

"I was a scientist here. I helped extract the ruthane and store it."

Seb didn't reply, waiting for more information.

"In my spare time I studied different races and species. I spent hours reading about them. There's only so much to do down here." Wilson stared into the darkness and spoke with a quieter voice, clearly trying to keep Hannah and Alison from hearing him. "I loved to travel. I only took this job when Hannah came along because it gave us stability. Those things become important when you have a baby." He sighed. "Sometimes it makes sense to give up on your dreams."

"Maybe when you get off this planet, you can do a bit more?"

"*If* we get off this planet."

"We will," Seb said. "So you know about the grubs because of your studies?"

"Yep. They seem consistent with many other hive-minded creatures I've learned about. I'm almost certain that killing the queen will also kill the grubs. And because they heal their host, hopefully your friend will be okay when she gets the dead thing out of her body."

"Hopefully," Seb said and glanced behind at the furious little Sparks again.

Before Seb could ask any more questions, SA tensed up in front of them. At the same time, Sparks whipped up into even more of a rage.

Wilson froze and Seb pushed him back to be with his wife and child. "Stay there," he said, and stepped towards SA.

Two steps forward and Seb heard the whoosh of grubs rushing over the soft ground towards them. He couldn't hear the footsteps of infected people. Maybe all the zombies were down.

With such limited visibility, Seb relied on his ears. The grubs sounded close, but not yet close enough to attack.

Sore eyes from refusing to blink, Seb's world slipped into slow motion, his heart pounding. A deep breath and he continued to watch the inky darkness in front of them. Any moment now and they'd be fighting what would hopefully prove to be the final wave of the vile things.

CHAPTER 44

Seb moved forward to be next to SA and stared down the tunnel. He still didn't hear any footsteps in the oncoming rush. That had to be a good thing, right? Every time he'd taken one of his kind down, it twisted the knife in his heart. Not that the *swoosh* of the grubs racing over the muddy ground offered any comfort.

Then Seb saw one. Several light bulbs down, it moved through the splash of light as it closed in on them.

Seb watched the lead grub plunge back into the shadow before he saw it in the next weak pool of light. Like a dolphin vanishing beneath the sea and then bursting from it again, the grub vanished and reappeared, getting closer every time he saw it.

When the lead worm went through the light closest to him, moving quickly despite Seb's slow-motion view of things, he darted forwards and slammed his foot down on it.

A rancid burst of rot shot up from the crushed creature. Although Seb screwed his face up in response to the stench, he focused on the sound of more worms to come.

SA took the next one out. Before Seb had a chance to say

anything, a carpet of the revolting things moved through the light farthest away from them. It looked like hundreds of the fat little beasts.

Seb ran forward and SA went with him. They needed distance between them and the others behind them. Together they both stamped on the grubs at the front, taking them down as quickly as they came forward.

Even with his world slowed down, Seb fought to keep up. Whenever he stamped on one, two replaced it. Sweat lifted beneath his clothes as his body temperature rose. Heavy breaths to keep up with the pace, he stamped on grub after grub.

As much as Seb wanted to check the others were okay, he couldn't. A lapse in concentration and they were screwed. The grubs would overwhelm them all.

To be sure he killed each one, Seb stamped down hard. Each pound of his foot against the ground sent a jolt up his legs. The ache from the repeated action balled as pain in his knees. But he kept going, each stamp returning the satisfying squelch of grub eradication.

A heave sat on the back of Seb's tongue. The smell mixed with his effort and the taste of bile lifted up in his throat. He swallowed it down and kept going.

Even as he fought, most of his attention on the grubs, Seb couldn't help but notice SA beside him. She moved like the wind, a rhythmic stamp against the ground as she took out grub after grub. She killed twice as many as he did. Even more impressive considering his gift gave him at least twice as much time to combat them.

CHAPTER 45

By the time Seb and SA had finished, the ground lay slick again with the grubs' clear sludge. A glistening surface, the weak light from the bulbs shimmered on it, making it look like ice on the dark ground.

When Seb looked over his shoulder at the others, he saw Wilson and his family were fine. Bruke still had a tight grip on Sparks, and Sparks seemed slightly calmer than she had a few moments before. Maybe the threat had passed for the moment. Although, she still looked like she wanted to tear into Wilson and his family. From the way Wilson kept looking over his shoulder at her, he knew it too.

"Right," Seb said, panting as he tried to get his words out. "That's the first threat neutralised. Hopefully that's all of them and we just have the queen left. How far until the end of this mine, Wilson?"

At first, Wilson simply raised a shaking finger as he pointed off down the tunnel. He finally got his words out. "Just around the corner."

SA led the way again and Seb let her. Why wouldn't he when he'd just seen her in action against the grubs?

It didn't take long for SA to stop again. She clearly had better sight than Seb because he couldn't make out what lay up ahead. Several steps past her and he too stopped in his tracks. "Wow! What is that thing?"

After he'd looked at SA, Seb then looked back at Wilson. "Come and see this, will ya?"

Hesitant at first, Wilson came over to Seb's side and stared at the end of the tunnel. "That's the queen," he said in a whisper.

"You sure?"

Wilson had turned pale and he nodded as he backed away. "Yep."

Although she looked like all of the other grubs, the queen sat about ten times larger than any they'd seen so far. Fat, pink, and the size of a domestic cat, she seemed to pulsate as she lay there next to the ruthane pipe.

On closer inspection, Seb saw the pulsing came from a writhing mass of unborn babies inside her. She'd been stretched so wide, he could see the grubs through her thin skin. When one popped out of her and rushed at them, SA flew past Seb and took it down with a heavy stamp.

Before Seb could do anything, SA ran forward, cut the queen open from top to bottom and stamped down on the grubs as they spilled out of her on a tide of what looked like amniotic fluid.

The smell of rot—worse than he'd smelled before—turned Seb's stomach. Wilson vomited behind them.

When SA had finished, Seb looked behind at Sparks. She still seemed agitated. More agitated than she'd been when near just Wilson and his family. They hadn't killed them all.

A scan of their surroundings and Seb turned in time to see a grub fly through the air at SA. One step to close the gap and he caught it mid-flight with a hard punch. It sent the fat little thing across the mine into a nearby wall.

The grub fell to the ground and SA stamped on it. She looked at Seb and dipped the slightest nod of thanks at him. Seb smiled back.

The sound of Sparks' fury left her. They'd clearly got all of them. Seb relaxed a little and turned to watch his small friend, waiting for her to change back into her normal self.

CHAPTER 46

Seb felt like he hadn't drawn breath for the last five minutes as he stared at Sparks, waiting for something to happen. Excitement had pushed his heart rate high from anticipating his friend's return.

But that excitement began to ebb as Sparks continued to snap at the air, biting in the direction of Wilson and his family. She looked as hungry to attack them now as she'd been the entire time they'd been around her for.

Grief clawed at Seb's throat to watch a palsied writhe twist through her small frame. Her eyes remained blood-red.

Seb couldn't help but look at Wilson now. From the way the man flinched, he seemed aware of the attention on him, but he didn't look back.

What had been butterflies of excitement in Seb's gut now burned in his stomach as if the fluttering creatures had razor-sharp wings. He couldn't hold it in any more. "So much for your theory."

Wilson opened and closed his mouth, shaking his head to the point where his chin wobbled beneath it. "I ... I ..."

"You're bloody useless is what you are. You've spent

your life studying species and you've learned *nothing*." Seb stepped closer to the man and balled his cold metal fists. "What possessed you to tell me we could help her? Why would you get my hopes up like that?"

At Seb's advance, Wilson stepped back. His attention on the ground, he said, "I'm sorry. It was only a theory."

"A theory you seemed pretty sure of."

Wilson sighed. "I was certain it would work."

When Seb moved towards the man another step, SA edged herself between them. It helped snap him from his need to destroy, but he still said, "I'm glad I don't have to rely on you for much. Not with that kind of certainty."

Before Wilson could say anything else, Seb walked off in the direction of the recreational area.

When Seb passed Bruke and saw his friend staring at him, he said, "Come on, let's get out of here."

Although he didn't look around again, Seb heard Bruke address Wilson. "I'm sorry about him. He's upset."

It took all Seb had not to shout at Bruke at that moment. Although SA had helped him see it wouldn't serve any purpose to attack Wilson, he had nothing to apologise for. Wilson had been wrong, not him.

CHAPTER 47

The others followed behind Seb as he walked back up the muddy tunnel, his feet turning beneath every purposeful stride on the damp ground. When he heard the footsteps of one of them running to catch up with him, his entire body tensed.

Wilson pulled level with Seb and fell into step beside him. "I'm sorry."

A deep breath and Seb let go of some of the tension in his body with a hard exhale. "It's okay. You've nothing to be sorry about. I got my hopes up and was upset when Sparks didn't turn back. I shouldn't have reacted the way I did."

Wilson didn't respond.

The bright lights of the recreational area shone down the dark tunnel. It made Seb feel like he could breathe more easily. Less like the walls were closing in around him. "But there *must* be some way to help her," he added.

Again, Wilson didn't say anything. Not that Seb could blame him. Especially after how he'd just reacted to him for getting his theory wrong. If he had any more theories, he'd probably keep them to himself from then on.

"Where do you think they came from?" Seb said.

"The grubs?"

"Yeah."

"You'll think I'm paranoid."

"Try me."

"Well, they came in through the hangar."

"From outside?"

"Yep. We've been here some time and we haven't seen anything living out there."

"It's hardly optimal conditions," Seb agreed.

"Exactly. Also, they arrived shortly after the Camorons announced to the galaxy that they'd discovered ruthane." A pause as Wilson looked at Seb and he lowered his voice. "And what it's worth."

"You think someone sent them down here?"

"In my experience, where there's credits, there's often corruption."

When they got closer to the doors leading through to the recreational area, Seb looked at the fallen bodies from their battle earlier and turned back to Wilson. "I'm sorry your daughter has to see this." He screwed his nose up at the rotten stench. "We didn't have the time or inclination to clear them away after we'd killed them. Had we known we'd be bringing a child back with us, we probably would have left these bodies elsewhere."

After Wilson had looked over his shoulder at his daughter, he returned his attention to Seb. "It's okay, she saw much worse when it all kicked off in the canteen. Better they're dead than alive with a parasite in them."

Seb looked at Wilson, and the chubby man clapped his hand to his mouth. "I'm so sorry. I didn't mean that. What I meant is—"

"It's okay, honestly." To look at Sparks as she fought

against Bruke's restraint weighed heavy on Seb. "She's in a bad way. I can see that. I just can't give up on her."

The conversation died between the pair and Seb returned his attention to where they were heading. The sooner they got out of the complex, the better.

CHAPTER 48

Seb emerged into the hangar first, sweating from the ascent up the large ladders. After checking to see the huge metal doors leading outside were still closed, he turned to watch Bruke climb the last few metres with the bound Sparks under his arm.

When Seb moved over to help his scaled friend, he winced from the aches in his body. It had been a long day. He took Sparks and restrained her while Bruke got himself up into the hangar.

Seb then passed Sparks straight back to him. Even someone of Sparks' size challenged his fatigued muscles at that moment. Thankfully they had Bruke. He'd struggled to climb the ladders on his own, let alone carrying Sparks up with him. Now they were up top, the scaled Bruke restrained her without any apparent struggle.

Not even out of breath, Bruke held Sparks in a strong grip, looked up, and said, "What?"

"You do everything you can to keep your strengths hidden. The effort that climb must have just taken …"

After looking down the hole he'd just climbed out of,

Bruke looked back at Seb and shrugged. "It was nothing really."

Seb laughed. "See what I mean? Modest to a fault."

Before Bruke could say anything else, Seb walked across the hangar to the tank where they'd left their suits. About thirty minutes had passed since he'd radioed in for someone to pick them up. "They'll be here soon," he said to the others.

"Who?" Wilson asked, his voice echoing in the large hangar.

"Our ride out of here."

The crack of a water bottle rang through the open space as Wilson took another sip of his drink. On their way back up, they'd stopped to get water in the canteen. Bruke had picked up some food too, but with the smell of the grubs in the air, Seb couldn't face any himself.

Before they'd gone to the canteen, they'd also picked up their weapons where they'd left them. They'd dragged the bodies free of the doors leading to the mines so they could seal the highly explosive ruthane in again. Although, with the doors open for as long as they had been, none of them felt confident using their blasters. Fortunately, the need hadn't arisen.

A clicking sound and Seb looked over to SA, who'd set the doors leading down into the mines to close. "Good idea," he said. They'd closed every set of doors behind themselves so far. "I'm sure with them sealed too, we don't need to worry about the ruthane anymore."

Once the hatch had closed, Wilson said, "Do you need radiation suits?"

A shake of his head and Seb pointed at the roof of the tank he now stood next to. "We have our own."

"How long do they last outside for?"

"Three hours."

"Three hours! Ours only last ninety minutes."

"That'll be plenty of time," Seb said. "We only need to get on the shuttle and get out of here."

Wilson led his family to a rail with radiation suits hanging from it while Seb pulled all the suits down from the tank. He thought of Sparks not being able to reach and smiled. Then he looked at her again, his mirth vanishing instantly. They'd get her back to her old self. They had to.

They took turns putting their suits on, passing the fitting and writhing Sparks between them so one of them could hold her while the others dressed. Seb had already put his suit on when he had to restrain her. Even though he'd only worn it for a short time, he'd started to get used to accommodating the thick layer surrounding him and gripped on tightly to his twisting friend. "You won't remain like this," he whispered to her, so quietly no one heard him. Or if they did, they didn't look up at him.

Bruke and SA were all suited up and Seb still had a hold of Sparks. "I suppose we have to dress her now?" he said.

Again, Bruke volunteered. Maybe Seb should have offered himself, but Bruke had more strength to hold onto her than Seb and SA combined.

Bruke wrapped his thick arms around Sparks and lifted her from the ground. SA held onto her thrashing legs and Seb slipped the suit over them. "Good job she's only small," he said as he fought against her squirming. "It's like dressing a child." Even now, with her in her current state, he couldn't help fishing for a reaction from her. She replied with the same fizzing and spitting chaos.

Despite her best efforts, Sparks couldn't do anything to stop the others from suiting her up. She was too small and weak, even with her rage driving her.

The struggle and the thickness of his own suit raised

Seb's body temperature. Sweat ran down the sides of his face. He wiped it away before pressing the button on the side of his head. The world in front of him turned slightly yellow as his visor slid across. Now finally suited up, Seb turned to see Wilson and his family were watching them.

"Impressive," Hannah said. Both her and her mum had been quiet in the mines, clearly recognising they should stay out of the way. But now they were safer, she'd obviously grown in confidence. Although not confident enough to prevent her face from turning crimson. She seemed aglow with childish nervousness at maybe making the wrong comment.

A smile and Seb said, "Thank you." Not that he needed praise on restraining his friend, he'd rather not have had to do it at all, but it seemed to lift the girl from her temporary anxiety.

The crackle of Sparks' radio rang out through the hangar and Seb looked at his small friend. "Damn it!" They'd sealed the radio inside her suit with her.

Just before Seb could move towards her, Bruke lifted the radio up. Seb smiled. "I'm glad one of us is on the ball."

A stoic nod and Bruke handed the radio over.

"Hello?" Seb said after he'd pressed the button on the side.

"Seb, we're nearly there. We're going to land just outside. Be ready, yeah?"

"Okay. See you soon."

The display on Seb's visor read '2h50m'. It would give him plenty of time outside, but it didn't help ease the tightening in his stomach at the thought of leaving the hangar for the radiated wasteland. But they had to get on. And he had to lead.

CHAPTER 49

Seb got to the hangar doors, swiped his keycard through the reader, and watched them open. At least they didn't have to hack into the computer controlling them. They'd have come up woefully short now they were without Sparks' abilities.

The increasing gap in the doors revealed the sprawling red wasteland beyond. Experience had told Seb not to expect it, but that didn't stop him wincing at the anticipated rush of hot air from outside.

The bodies from the first wave of zombies they'd fought stretched out before them. They'd only been dead a short while, but Carstic's vicious atmosphere had already turned their skin yellow and their eyes had sunk into their faces. It looked like the air had leeched the life from them, mummifying them in the short time they'd been exposed for. Many of the bodies had visible wounds where they'd shot the parasites before they could crawl from their mouths. Their scabs were now black as if they'd been burned.

When Seb checked on Hannah, he saw Alison talking to her as they walked. Not only dead bodies, but dead bodies of the people they once knew. The girl seemed to understand her mother's intention and kept her focus on her.

A few seconds later, the rush of engines called out to them. Seb looked up to see the shuttle flying towards them. "You ready?" he said to Wilson, Hannah, and Alison. All three of them nodded, relief lifting their exhausted faces.

∼

SEB LED THE WAY TO MEET THE LANDING SHUTTLE. HE looked over the wasteland but couldn't see any threats. Why would there be? It was a dead planet. Although, Wilson *had* theorised that the parasites came from outside.

The shuttle seemed to agitate Sparks more than ever and she twisted and shook in Bruke's grip. Seb chewed on his bottom lip as he looked at her. "They won't let us on the shuttle with her in that state. Can you do anything to subdue her?"

Bruke shook his head.

As the shuttle drew close, the thrust from the engines buffeted Seb's suit and sent him stumbling back a step. Sparks became even more animated.

"Do something, Bruke." But Seb could see Bruke already doing everything he could, his teeth clenched as he battled against Sparks' movement.

The shuttle landed and SA helped Bruke restrain Sparks. She fought against them with more vigour than Seb had seen from her before. She thrashed and twisted, seemingly desperate to get at the people on the shuttle.

The shuttle door opened and a large creature from the Shadow Order stared at them. It had a round blue face twice the size of Seb's. It had thick and waxy skin. "What's wrong with her?" it said.

"She's got a parasite in her."

"We're not taking her."

Tiredness got the better of Seb and he snapped. While pointing a finger at the beast, he said, "Don't tell me what you're not going to do, you ugly toad."

"What did you call me?" The creature's shoulders lifted and he balled his large fists.

A sigh and Seb let go of his anger. No fear when it came to a potential fight with the creature, but if Seb were in his situation, then he'd probably refuse Sparks entry to the shuttle too. What would Moses do to the creature who brought her back to the Shadow Order's base in that state? "Sorry," he said, "that was uncalled for. But we're not leaving her here. We need to try to help her."

Before the beast could reply, Bruke pulled on Seb's sleeve. At first he shrugged it off, returning his attention to the creature, but when Bruke pulled on it again, Seb spun around and said, "What?"

It took for Seb to follow the line where Bruke pointed to see the things coming towards them. A squint to see better through his visor—the time reading '2h45m'—and he saw their blood-red eyes. "Shit!"

CHAPTER 50

The two beasts were huge. Easily the size of fully grown elephants, they were shaped like seals. As pink as newborn moles, they ran across the open wasteland. Despite their clumsy gait—their heads bobbing up and down as they ran while their bottoms moved the opposite way like a nodding donkey—they ate away at the distance between them and the shuttle quicker than their forms should have been capable of.

And their eyes. Seb couldn't look away from them. The blood-red of beings infected with the parasites. The blood-red that stared back at him through Sparks' visor in her radiation suit despite the yellow tint. The blood-red that lusted after destruction.

Seb raised the stock of his gun to his shoulder. One eye closed, he looked down the barrel of it. His world slowed down as he ripped off several green blasts.

They flew over the red rocky wasteland and sailed harmlessly wide of the monsters. The distance alone made it hard to hit the huge creatures. Their unusual lolling run made it damn near impossible to draw a bead on them.

"Quick," Seb shouted at Wilson and his family. "Get on the shuttle now."

They didn't need to be told twice. As they clambered into the back, the toad-like soldier reached out of the shuttle and helped them on.

SA moved next to Seb. It felt like she understood what had to happen. Calm stillness, it felt like she was telling him she'd follow him wherever he needed to go.

Because Sparks didn't need her weapons at that moment, SA had taken both of her blasters. As quick as an automatic rifle, she sent shots across the wasteland at the creatures. She missed with every one. Much closer than Seb had managed, but still nowhere near taking them down. They'd have to let them get closer. But how close before they were committing suicide?

Maybe SA had given Seb her silent support like he'd thought, but maybe he'd misinterpreted her. Either way, he needed his friends more now than ever. "Follow me," he called out as he turned away from the shuttle and ran back towards the hangar.

"What are you doing?" Bruke shouted after him, frozen to the spot as he looked between Seb and their ride out of there.

"No time to explain," Seb shouted back. "But you need to come. And bring Sparks. They won't let her on the shuttle and I think I know how to save her."

SA and Bruke ran after Seb. Bruke had thrown Sparks over his shoulder and moved as if she weighed nothing.

The sound of the shuttle's engines rumbled behind them, and just before Seb got to the hangar, he heard the ship take off again.

The hangar doors were wide open, so Seb ran through them straight to the keycard reader. He swiped his card through the slot to close them.

Seb watched both SA and Bruke run through the closing doors into the hangar. Bruke put Sparks down and restrained her again.

As the doors closed, Seb watched the creatures descend on them. Strange things, they made a noise somewhere between a trumpet and a roar as they got closer. But they wouldn't make it through the doors before they closed. They were quick, but not that quick.

The doors pinched out the last strip of daylight as Seb heard the whir of the shuttle's guns outside. He listened as a meteor shower of blasts crashed against the rocky ground. He felt the vibration of them through the soles of his feet.

The trumpeting roar of the creatures fell silent.

When the light above the hangar doors turned green, Seb pressed the button on the side of his head and watched the world return to its normal hue. He listened as Bruke and SA breathed heavily from the run. That and Sparks' snarling fury. He looked at Bruke and SA and spoke through his laboured breaths. "I think they got them."

SA moved over to one of the small windows in the hangar doors before she looked back at Seb and nodded. Bruke continued to battle with Sparks.

Seb jumped when the radio hissed from his top pocket. He pulled it free and pressed the talk button on the side. "Did you get them?"

"Yes," the creature who wouldn't let Sparks on the shuttle said. "Both of them are down. But never mind that. *What* are you doing?"

"We couldn't leave," Seb said. "There are more infected creatures. More parasites that need to be taken down. That *is* our mission, after all."

Wilson's voice came through the receiver at him. "Are you thinking the creature in the mines wasn't the main queen?" The rumble of the shuttle in flight roared as a background noise behind the scientist.

"There are obviously more beasts on Carstic than you originally thought," Seb said. "From the look of it, they've also been infected by the parasites. We have to kill *all* of the grubs."

"And maybe help Sparks in the process?"

"Hopefully."

Bruke and SA watched Seb the entire time.

"And maybe it'll explain why the grubs came from out of the wastelands," Seb added.

"Maybe," Wilson said, although he didn't sound convinced.

"Maybe the grubs weren't planted here by someone looking to get at the Camorons' wealth in some way."

Wilson didn't reply.

Seb leaned against the wall with the card reader on it. In a strange way, it felt good to see the huge pink beasts. It meant there might be a queen of the hive mind they were yet to take down. It also meant the grubs weren't put on the planet. They'd probably lived there the entire time. It meant the Camorons weren't being used for their wealth. Because, at the end of the day, if anyone was using the Camorons to get rich, it would most likely be Moses and, by extension, them.

CHAPTER 51

The radio burst back to life, startling Seb and making him jump away from the wall. Wilson's voice came through. "There's a lush area a few miles from the hangar. It's like a rainforest. Green, damp, vibrant ..."

Seb waited for him to say more, watching Bruke and SA as they too listened in.

"Kind of hard to believe on a planet so barren. If you come out of the hangar and head in a straight line, you'll get to it."

"And what's there?"

"We don't know."

"But you know it's there?"

"We've been there, but we only had ninety-minute radiation suits, so we couldn't stay long."

"Ninety minutes wasn't enough time?"

"No, we could only go in so far with that. The place is huge," Wilson said.

"How do you know it's big?"

"We've seen it from satellite images, but we've never seen any life in there, which is why we assumed it didn't have any. Our satellites can take a photo of a flea's arse anywhere on this planet."

"So where did those two beasts come from?"

"I don't know."

"Okay, so that's where we'll go. How good is the tank in here? Will it get us to the rainforest?"

"It's amazing," Wilson said. "It'll get you there in no time and keep the radiation off you. As long as it's all sealed up, you'll be fine to travel in it for as long as you need to. You can open the doors and close them again and it'll clear the radiation in seconds."

"And you still didn't have enough time to explore the forest when you travelled there in the tank?"

"Like I said, the forest is huge."

Both SA and Bruke continued to watch Seb. Neither showed any signs of objecting to the plan yet. "Okay, thank you for all your help."

"Thank you for saving my family."

Seb didn't reply.

"Oh, and Seb?"

"Yeah?"

"I didn't say anything before."

"About what?"

"About you."

A look at the other two and Seb said, "What about me?"

"You're human."

"Yep."

"But you're not. I can see that in you. There's something else. Something much greater than human."

"What are you talking about?"

The radio hissed at Seb and the line went dead. "Wilson?"

Nothing.

"Wilson?"

Just the hiss of the radio.

"They must have a problem with their radio," Bruke said, grimacing as he continued to fight against Sparks.

"You reckon?"

A frown and Bruke pulled his head back. "There's no need to be facetious."

"Sorry," Seb said. "The radio cut off at a frustrating time. I shouldn't take it out on you."

"We'll see Wilson again," Bruke said.

"Yeah." Seb nodded. "I'll talk to him then. For now, we need to get to the lush part of the planet he was talking about. It looks like we have more grubs to take down."

Seb turned the dial on Sparks' radio to change the channel. "I need to call Moses and tell him what's happening."

CHAPTER 52

A knot of anxiety sat in Seb's guts. He hated talking to Moses, especially when he had to defer to him. The large shark-like creature claimed to always be available on channel six, so he switched it to channel six and pressed the button on the side of the radio. "Moses, it's Seb."

"Seb, I was hoping you'd call. What's happening down there?"

He'd obviously spoken to the shuttle, but Seb humoured him anyway. "We've cleared the mining complex out."

"Good work."

"But as we were leaving, more creatures appeared."

"And?"

"*Infected* creatures."

"So it's not just contained to the mines?"

"No, there are more parasites on Carstic."

"That's why you didn't get on the shuttle?" Before Seb could reply, Moses explained, "The crew on the shuttle were telling me everything, but we've lost contact with them."

"Yeah, us too."

"Do you think you can save Sparks?"

The small Thrystian twisted and shook against Bruke's grip as she continued to try to work her way free. A heavy sigh and Seb said, "I hope so." To look at her in her current state tore at his heart.

"Just don't bring her back here if she's infected with one of those *things*."

"I'm not letting her die, Moses."

"She *isn't* coming to Aloo with a parasite in her."

Seb replied through gritted teeth, "I'm *not* letting her die."

A moment's pause, and Moses said, "Let's cross that bridge if we have to."

They needed to move forward. It wouldn't do them any good to argue. "The dad of the family we rescued," Seb said, "has a theory that the parasites have a queen. That if we kill the queen, all the others will die."

"And you trust him?"

"I'm not sure, but we've got to try, right? I mean, we have to take the parasites down anyway."

Another moment of radio static where Moses didn't reply.

"He has another theory too."

"Oh?"

"He thinks the grubs were put on the planet to clear the mine out. That someone wanted the complex clear so they could get to the ruthane. But I think that's been disproven now we've seen that other creatures are zombies too. That the parasites were probably outside all along. But I wonder if there's any weight to it?"

"It seems a bit far-fetched. I know ruthane's expensive, but he sounds like a conspiracy theory nut."

"I suppose nearly dying of thirst in a small cave would do that to you. I hope he's right about the queen though."

"Me too." Moses sounded like he wanted to repeat to Seb that he couldn't bring Sparks back, but he didn't. Instead, he pulled in a long breath and said, "Good luck, and see you when you get back."

Just talking to Moses made Seb's blood boil. He'd never been good with authority, especially authority he had zero respect for. A million snarky comments flashed through his mind, but before he could say a single one of them, a loud explosion burst through the air outside. The shock of it rumbled through the ground.

Seb looked at SA, who'd remained by the window in the hangar doors. She looked back at him with wide eyes and an open mouth.

Because she couldn't tell him any more than that, Seb ran over to the window and looked out at the large cloud of grey smoke. "The shuttle?"

When SA nodded, Seb let out a long sigh. He looked back at the vast cloud of smoke and shook his head. "Damn."

CHAPTER 53

Weakened by what he saw outside, Seb leaned against the large metal doors for support. A jumble of words sat inside his head, but he couldn't grasp the form of them.

After several deep breaths, Seb had pulled himself together enough to call Moses back on the radio. Before Moses had a chance to speak, he said, "What just happened?"

Clearly irked by Seb's directness, Moses paused for a few seconds and breathed heavily into the microphone. He then replied in a low tone as if holding back his fury. "What are you talking about?"

"The shuttle!"

"What about the shuttle?"

Such a tight grip on the radio, Seb heard the plastic casing crack a little. He eased off. His new hands were much more capable of crushing things than his old ones. He had to remember that. "The shuttle with Wilson and his family just blew up as it was flying away. What happened?"

A pause before Moses said, "I'm ... I'm not sure." After

another pause, he came back on the radio. "I can't get through to anyone to find out."

"I'm not surprised," Seb said, "considering they were all just cremated out there."

Another monotone reply came back at him. "You'll have to leave it with me."

What could Seb say to that? Far from satisfactory, but if Moses didn't know anything, he couldn't tell him anything. No point in replying, Seb let go of the talk button and put the radio back in his pocket.

When Seb finally looked up, he met the penetrative stare of SA and shrugged. "Your guess is as good as mine," he said.

Even though Bruke stood a few metres away from them, still holding onto Sparks and wrestling to keep her under control, he stood close enough to hear the conversation with Moses. Hard not to in the near silent hangar. "Let's just hope the shuttle wasn't powered by ruthane, and if it was, that the explosion had nothing to do with the gas." He looked at the tank. "That thing's probably loaded with the stuff." After he'd looked around the hangar, he added, "And I don't think anything else will get us to the rainforest."

A look at the large black tank and Seb sighed. "I hadn't thought of that."

Seb looked at Sparks again, the now familiar twist of pain spasming through her. "I'm going to take it anyway. I want to do everything I can to save Sparks. I don't expect either of you to come with me. It's a choice you need to make."

Every time Bruke shrugged, it highlighted just how broad his shoulders were. "I'll go wherever you do, Seb," he said.

When Seb looked at SA, he saw no sign of hesitation when she nodded at him.

"Okay," Seb said, "I'll drive. SA, can you get on the turret?"

SA nodded again.

One last look at Sparks, her fitting as vehement as ever, and Seb said, "Let's do this."

CHAPTER 54

The second they left the hangar, they found the remains of the two beasts that had chased them. As Seb manoeuvred the tank around their huge pink corpses, he looked down to see they were riddled with holes from where the shuttle had torn into them. Blue blood pooled around them, and a grub—easily the size of the queen they'd found in the mines—lay dead by each corpse. Thankfully they didn't have to wait for the fat things to crawl out so they could kill them. It wouldn't be that plain sailing for the rest of their journey.

The vast expanse of red wasteland stretched out in front of Seb. He saw it as slightly orange because of the yellow tint to his visor. It made sense for him to drive. If the tank moved as quickly as they thought it might, his slow-motion view of things would help.

After a deep breath, the tank's engine purring through the machine, Seb called back to the others. "You ready?"

"Hang on," Bruke said as he tied another strap around Sparks. They'd already secured her to her seat, but they wanted to make sure she couldn't get free. Especially as Bruke would have to be the one to restrain her again.

After he'd pulled the strap tight, Bruke looked up at SA on the turret and then back at Seb. He nodded. "Okay, let's do this."

Seb stamped down on the accelerator and the tank took off. Pinned back in his seat, their velocity switched on his ability to see the world in slow motion.

It took just seconds for the tank's hard tyres to send a tooth-loosening rattle through the vehicle. They were tough, able to deal with any terrain, but because they had no air in them, their lack of absorption made for a bumpy ride.

The rattle through the tank blurred Seb's vision and he had to use his strengthened grip just to hold on to the shaking wheel. But they moved like they would break the land speed record. No wonder everyone wanted to get their hands on ruthane.

CHAPTER 55

The landscape continued to shoot past them and Seb felt like he hadn't blinked for the past ten minutes. His eyes burned as he watched the slightly orange blur outside the tank's windscreen. As much as he focused on the horizon, he hadn't yet seen the rainforest Wilson had talked about. Clearly, it was more than a few miles away. He drew a deep sigh. Poor Wilson.

Then Seb saw them: three huge pink blobs. Just before he could shout up to SA, a thick green shot burst from the turret on top of the tank. She missed.

Three large creatures like the ones they'd seen outside the hangar. Because they were moving towards one another, the gap between the tank and the beasts closed quickly. Too quickly. SA shot again and this time she hit one. Where their blasters had been ineffective, the green cannon bolt sank into one of the beast's heads, vaporising it.

"Good work, SA," Seb shouted back into the tank, his voice wavering with the vehicle's vibrations. The creature had no head and neck left. "That must have taken out the grub too."

Two more shots and SA dropped the other two. She'd clearly found her aim.

"Woot!" Seb shouted through the ship, his foot still pressed to the floor as he swerved to avoid the pink bodies. "Well done!"

Before the echo of Seb's shout had died down, he saw the others. He slumped in his seat. "Damn!"

They must have only taken down the front-runners. A line of creatures at least twenty wide stretched across Seb's view.

SA sent more blasts into the beasts. Several more large explosions of blue mist. Several more of the beasts tripped and fell. She had this, Seb didn't need to worry.

But then the shots stopped.

After a few seconds of no blasts—the creatures and the tank getting closer to one another—Seb called behind him again. "Bruke, go up there and see what's happening."

Despite the rattle of the tank going over the hard ground, Seb could just about hear Bruke shout, "What's going on, SA?"

Hard to listen in on a one-sided conversation and drive the tank. Especially as Seb's slowed-down perspective dragged out every one of Bruke's syllables.

Despite his overwhelming urge to stop and go back to investigate, Seb had to trust they'd sort it out between them. They needed him behind the wheel.

No more than about fifty metres separated the tank and the creatures now. At least fifteen of them left, the powerful vehicle could probably mow down one or two, but not the wall of pink in front of them. The immovable objects undermined what Seb had seen as their unstoppable force.

"What's going on?" Seb called back, his stinging eyes on the beasts in front of them.

No reply.

"Sod it," Seb said, came off the accelerator and pressed the brake. A pounding heart, he gripped the gear stick with his sweating hand and shoved it into reverse. Then he waited, stationary in the middle of the red wasteland.

"The cannon's overheated," Bruke finally said. The tank's growling engine sounded out as the only background noise now they'd stopped moving.

Bruke then said, "It's cooling down now."

About twenty metres between the tank and the beasts.

"How long?" Seb asked.

No reply.

Ten metres.

Still nothing from Bruke.

Seb saw the monster's red eyes fix on him. Their shaking stampede sent vibrations through his seat. A twitching foot, and Seb tried again. "How long, Bruke?"

Still no reply.

Just a few metres away, Seb slammed the accelerator down. The tank shot backwards just as one of the lead beasts roared and leapt at them. It missed, crashing down on the rocky ground where the tank had been only moments before.

Seb gripped the wheel as tightly as he had when going forward. The monsters kept pace with him for the first few metres, but he slowly increased the gap between them.

The rumble of the uneven ground vibrated through Seb's hands. He had to hold the steering wheel straight. Sweat leaked from his brow and ran into his already sore eyes. He listened to his own panic in his rapid breaths; smelled his own perspiration. Whatever happened, he had to hold them straight. Any slight twitch and they'd lose control.

"How long?" Seb shouted again. The beasts were still close to them.

Nothing.

Such a tight grip, Seb felt the galvanised rubber steering wheel give in to his pressure. He loosened his squeeze a little as they passed the three beasts they'd killed first. Thankfully they didn't crash into them. "Bruke, *how long?*"

Still no more than ten metres between Seb and the fastest beast. They were losing them, but very, very slowly. He stared into its red eyes, its bald snout, its almost featureless face as it bobbed up and down with its unusual gait. The thing was still so close to them he could almost see the pores in its skin. He could almost smell it through the glass screen in front of him.

An explosion of blue mist made Seb jump. The creature he'd just been looking at vanished behind the inky spray on his windscreen. A thud ran through the ground as it crashed down. The beast's blood on the windshield made it almost impossible to see the others behind it.

The pulse of another shot rang out above him. Through the blue mess in front of him, Seb only saw the silhouette of another creature fall. Then another pulse, each one kicking a hard recoil through the reversing tank.

What must have been seven or eight shots went off and Seb slowed down a little. He could only reverse for so long before he lost control. As he squinted through the blue mess in front of him, he saw more silhouettes. SA continued to rip off shots. Between each one, she paused longer than before. It must have been her way of stopping the cannon from overheating.

Five more shots and SA stopped.

"How are we doing up there?" Seb asked.

"All down," Bruke finally replied.

Seb eased off the accelerator and let the tank roll to a stop. When he let go of the steering wheel, he saw the imprint of his grip still on it.

"What's going on down there?" Bruke called out.

For a second, Seb said nothing as he looked at the windscreen and the blue blood coating it. "I can't see anything," he said. He stood up from his seat. "I need to go outside and wipe the windscreen. Make sure you've got my back." Although confident SA had blown all their heads and necks off, he added, "And watch out for those damn grubs."

CHAPTER 56

Seb gave Sparks a wide berth on his way to the tank's exit. The small Thrystian twisted and spat, growling at him as he got close to her. Hard when it hurt to see her in such a state, he did his best to ignore her anyway, and pressed the button next to the tank's door to open it.

The hatch lifted with a *whoosh* and Seb stepped out onto the barren planet, flinching at the expected rush of heat. Again, the rush didn't come. Hopefully he'd never get used to that. They needed off Carstic well before its quirks became familiar to him.

Red rock stretched away from Seb in every direction. Other than the tank and the fallen bodies of the creatures, he saw nothing.

A sudden wave of gratitude ran through Seb. The windscreen might have been coated in blood, but at least they hadn't broken down. There weren't many recovery services in this corner of the galaxy. He checked his top pocket for the radio and he found it there—just in case he needed to call Moses.

As Seb walked around to the front of the tank, he eyed the

headless and neckless creatures. SA had bullseyed every one of them. He looked up at the turret. Both SA and Bruke stared back at him through the clear dome that sat on top of the vehicle like a pimple.

The creature's blood looked even worse from the outside. Blue and thick, it clung to the front of the tank like tar. Thankfully the suit prevented Seb from smelling anything; the creature's insides probably stank.

Because Seb didn't have a cloth, he used his gloved hand to wipe the screen.

The blood had an oily quality, streaking across the glass every time Seb tried to clear it. No matter how many times he wiped, he still couldn't see through the windscreen.

Just before Seb could go back into the tank to find something to wipe it down with, a heavy blast shook the ground. SA had shot at him.

"What was that for?" Seb shouted as he looked up at the turret.

Even if SA had been able to speak, he wouldn't have heard her through the glass dome.

A chill crawled up Seb's spine. Whatever SA's reason, the situation had turned sour. She wouldn't shoot without good cause. Despite his reluctance to do so, he turned around. He then gasped, steaming his visor up temporarily. He'd already seen them, a wave of fat grubs rushing straight at him.

CHAPTER 57

Easily the size of sheep, the bugs were larger than any Seb had seen. They rushed at him in a wave of fat and pulsating horror.

Another green bolt flew over Seb's head and another bug exploded when the shot connected. It would seem it took more than blowing the heads and necks off the creatures to kill the parasites inside them. Maybe they settled in different parts of their host's anatomy depending on what species they took over. Maybe these parasites had very little to do with the ones they'd seen in the mines. What they'd learned so far could be useless.

Seb returned to the windscreen and rubbed quicker than before, his right shoulder aching from the effort of trying to clear his view. It spread the oil around the glass surface but not a lot else. He redoubled his efforts. SA would keep him safe. He had to trust that.

Shots continued to fly over Seb's head. Each one exploded closer behind him. When a shot hit the ground not far from his heels, the goo from the inside of the bug splattered his back with such force it thrust him against the tank.

Seb used his hands to brace against the windshield. When he pulled away, he saw the blood had cleared a little where he'd been pressing. The bug's bodily fluids had cut through the greasy oil.

Seb cleared the screen with renewed vigour, biting down on his bottom lip while he rubbed as hard as he could.

When he'd wiped a spot large enough to see out of—the blasts continuing to fly over him—Seb looked behind again. He wished he hadn't.

Spurred on by the sight, Seb ran away from the grubs around to the the back of the tank so he could re-enter it. He dived into the vessel, gasping for breath as he slapped the red button to close the tank's door.

The door seemed to take forever. It slowly rose while SA continued to rip off shots from the cannon.

Sparks fitted with more vigour, the appearance of the grubs clearly riling her. Screaming, shaking, and foaming at the mouth, she fought against her restraints and the entire tank shook with her movement.

The *whoosh* of the fat bugs slithered over the rocky ground as they got closer to the tank, but just before they reached it, the door clicked shut. A smattering of fat bodies slammed against the now closed door and Sparks turned to watch it, something akin to hope on her face as if she expected them to break through and free her.

After a double-check to be sure the door remained locked, Seb returned to the driver's seat. The reading on his screen showed his suit had 2h35m left. The three hours had seemed like a good amount of time when they'd landed. Now it seemed woefully inadequate.

Still able to see from the gap he'd wiped in the windscreen, Seb waited for a pause in SA's cannon shots. He shouted up at her and Bruke, "Right, let's get out of here."

As Seb moved forward, the grubs returned to the front of the tank like he'd hoped they would. They threw themselves against the screen, their fat bodies hitting the glass and sliding down it.

Rather than hindering him, they actually helped wipe the screen clear, especially when SA shot one as it jumped towards the vehicle. Its explosion of fluids sprayed the screen and cut through the grease.

The pop of the grubs snapped through the tank when Seb ran them over. The hard tyres made light work of their fat bodies. Between him and SA, they could kill them all without having to go outside again.

As they picked up speed, the rush of adrenaline settled within Seb. His tired arms shook and his breathing eased. At least they were safe inside the tank. Although, when they got to where they were heading, no doubt they'd have to get out of it again.

But he couldn't think about that. He'd deal with it when he got there.

CHAPTER 58

"It's hard to see through the trees," Bruke said as he appeared next to Seb, bobbing and weaving as if his strange motion would improve his vision.

Seb couldn't see much either through the dense vegetation. The shock of lush green in front of them stood in stark contrast to everything they'd seen of Carstic so far. Not even the yellow tint of his visor could dull it. Vibrant, alive, and clearly damp like a rainforest. Despite having his suit on, he could almost feel the humidity of the place. "All of Carstic's water must be concentrated in this small area."

"Small?" Bruke said.

The forest loomed over them as they stood in front of it. It stretched away from them on both sides. So far Seb couldn't see either edge. He shrugged. "Relatively small compared to the miles of arid rock surrounding it."

Bruke looked over his shoulder at the locked-up tank behind them. "It's a shame we have to leave our early warning system behind. Do you think she'll be all right on her own?"

The question sent a snap of tension through Seb's gut. It

hadn't been an easy decision to leave Sparks tied up in the tank. The reading on his suit's visor said '2h30m'. Not an insignificant amount of time to leave her for. "I hope so," he finally said and shared an anxious look with SA. "I hope so."

Silence followed Seb's words as the three of them stared into the forest again.

Seb finally said, "I mean, what other choice do we have? We're doing this to help her, and we all need to be on hand to fight those things. She may give us an early warning, but she'll also slow us down. Have you seen the size of the monsters we have to fight? What if there's something even deadlier in there?"

It clearly didn't do much to calm Bruke down. The stocky creature moved from side to side, shifting his weight from one foot to the other as he held his gun with a tight grip.

The silence hung between them again and Seb looked back into the forest. On a sparse, dry, and barren planet, it stood as an oasis of life. The trees were taller than any he'd ever seen. Although, despite their vibrancy, they had to be the ugliest trees he'd seen too. Lumps littered their trunks like tumours. Thick bracken gathered at the base of them. Red and brilliant blue, it cluttered the ground. At some points it stood over six feet tall.

"The queen has to be in there somewhere," Seb said. "I just hope she's close by. We need to get this done for Sparks' sake if nothing else."

Seb lifted his semi-automatic blaster as he looked across at the other two. The timer on his screen had ticked down to '2h28m'. "Right, let's do this. You both ready?"

Not that Seb needed to ask SA, who raised her blaster. A few seconds later, Bruke nodded and did the same. SA had only taken one of Sparks' blasters this time, leaving the other one in the tank with her—for what good it would do.

"Okay." Seb stepped forward into the lush green forest, pushing through the bracken to enter the place. Condensation formed on his visor for the briefest second before he heard a click in his helmet and the mist cleared. Thankfully their suits were smart enough to deal with the hostile environment. Hopefully they were too.

CHAPTER 59

No more than two steps into the forest and Seb stopped. He looked at SA and Bruke. "Did you hear that?"

Before Bruke could answer, the sound came again. Louder than before. The rip and pop of snapping branches and the whoosh of bracken as something raced through it. Something large. Something heading straight for them.

The thunder of footsteps shook through the soft ground. They were close, but because of the densely packed trees, Seb couldn't see them yet.

A quickened pulse and shorter breaths, Seb saw the world in slow motion. He raised his blaster and looked down the barrel of it, doing his best to remain calm and keep himself steady.

A quick glance at SA and Bruke, and they both had their weapons ready to go too. They pointed them in the same direction as him.

By the time Seb saw the pink bobbing head, no more than about ten metres separated them. He ripped off a line of shots at the brute, but it did nothing to slow it down. Each green blast hit the monster's thick hide. It looked like the beast didn't even feel it as it continued to charge.

As hard as Seb focused, he couldn't see the thing's weak spot. A huge clumsy creature, it came towards him like a train.

Both SA and Bruke unloaded on the beast too with the same result as Seb. Their guns wouldn't get through its thick skin.

Already out of ideas, Seb winced as his gun shook in his hands. They were about to fall at the first hurdle.

CHAPTER 60

They had no other choice. Sure, the time in their radiation suits would run out, but the only thing that might save them now would be a retreat. Seb opened his mouth to shout the order, but then he saw it. The yellow tint to his visor must have dulled his gift in some way, but now the creature had got closer—too damn close—he saw the slightest shimmer above its blood-red eyes.

"Aim for its forehead," Seb shouted at the others, "just above its eyes."

It had got to within a few metres of them when SA took a shot at the beast. It sank deep into the spot Seb had identified. A puff of blue blood, the creature tripped, fell, and hit the ground so hard, it felt like the vibrations could topple the trees around them.

But they had no time to gather their thoughts. Where one of the beasts had fallen, three more appeared behind it. Seb, SA, and Bruke opened fire again.

The most accurate of the three, it still took SA several shots to drop the now closest monster, its bobbing head hard to hit as it charged forward.

Seb sent a barrage of blasts at the next one, the heat indicator on his gun already turning a deep orange.

Just a few metres left and probably no more shots, Seb hit the creature in the forehead. It tripped and fell like the other two had.

Although Bruke had adopted Seb's scattershot method, he didn't look anywhere near to taking down the last one.

The trumpeting roar of the creature shook the foliage around them. The beast ran straight at Bruke, about to take him down. Then SA hit it with a crack shot. Bruke flinched away from the spray of blood and then jumped aside to avoid being gathered up in its clumsy topple.

It took a few seconds for Seb to regain his senses over the pounding of his pulse, but as he listened, he couldn't hear any more creatures. He ignored the buzz in his hands urging him to bend down and help the brutes. Maybe they were a passive race, taken over like the humans had been in the mines. Maybe they deserved saving, but he couldn't fix the dead. If he could, Gurt would be beside them at that moment, and the creatures wouldn't have got anywhere near to them.

After he'd cleared his throat in the hope it would also clear the memory of Gurt, Seb said, "At least they're big. We may not be able to see them coming, but we can certainly hear them."

"What if some of the smaller grubs are in here too?" Bruke said.

Before responding to him, Seb looked at SA and she looked back. "I can't think about that," he said. "We'll deal with it if we have to."

"But we won't see them coming."

"Let's not create problems, yeah?" Seb said, and before Bruke could respond, he added, "We need to wait for the

grubs to come out of these things and then we can push on."
The radiation reading on his suit had dropped to '2h25m'.

CHAPTER 61

Fortunately the grubs inside the large creatures were much easier to kill than the creatures themselves. Four of them, they were easily the size of a small farm animal each, just like the ones they'd met out in the desert. They slid from their hosts' mouths and met a laser blast for their troubles. Each one exploded, their fat, liquid bodies popping like lanced boils.

By the time they were done, Seb and the other two were covered in slime from the vile creatures. Were it not for their radiation suits, the smell would undoubtedly be unbearable. Just the sight of the sludge as he wiped it from his view made him slightly nauseated.

Before they moved off again, Seb looked at the numbers on his visor. Hopefully they all had the same time. "Bruke, what's your radiation reading?"

"Just over two hours and ten minutes," Bruke said.

SA nodded with a slight shrug. She clearly had about that time too.

"Me too," Seb said. "This is far from a master plan, but I reckon we should walk in a straight line for fifty-five minutes and hope we come across the queen in that time. If we don't, we'll have to turn around and come back. Unless either of you have a better plan?"

Both Bruke and SA shook their heads.

"Bruke, you lead the way," Seb said.

At first, Bruke froze. Then he shook his head again. "I don't think that's a good idea. What if I can't kill one of the creatures when they spring us. I don't have the reactions of you and SA."

"We're right behind you," Seb said. "If a creature springs you, it springs all of us."

"I don't want to do it."

"Which is why you need to. Being brave isn't about not being scared. Being brave is feeling the fear and doing it anyway. Come on, Bruke, you're in the Shadow Order now, you need to lead once in a while."

Bruke straightened his posture, gripped his weapon, and nodded at Seb.

Seb and SA shared a look as Bruke strode off into the deep brush, pushing the blue and red bracken aside to get through it.

SA looked back at Seb as if to question his decision. But he stood by it. Bruke needed to get braver.

The *crack* of splitting rock took Seb's focus away from the ethereal bioluminescence of SA's attention.

Where Bruke had been a second before, there now sat a huge hole in the ground.

CHAPTER 62

Seb and SA rushed through the vibrant bracken to the edge of the hole Bruke had fallen into. It dropped down about five metres at the most. Not far. At least, it wouldn't have been far had Bruke not landed on a large cluster of rocks. He squirmed and twisted from where he'd clearly hurt himself.

What looked like a stream sprang from the rocks. Just a few metres farther along, it turned into a wide river. When Seb looked at SA and saw her still staring down into it, he said, "I suppose we've found where the water for this place comes from."

When Bruke sat up, he reached across and grabbed his left arm with his right hand. A wince crushed his face as he stared up in their direction. Despite the distance separating them, Seb's hands tingled with his desire to get down to him. To be fair to Bruke, he looked like he wanted to scream, but he held it in.

"We need to help him," Seb said, sitting on the edge of the hole before slipping down to their friend.

Soundless as ever, SA landed next to Seb when he reached the rocks.

Seb kneeled down beside Bruke and picked up his arm.

"Ow," Bruke said and pulled in a sharp breath through his clenched teeth. Tears glistened in his brown eyes, but he hadn't cried yet.

The buzz in Seb's hands nearly rendered them useless as he lifted his friend's arm and cupped where he sensed the injury to be.

In a matter of seconds, the twisted grimace of pain left Bruke's face and he stared in awe at Seb. He spoke as he exhaled relief. "Thank you."

After a nod at his friend, Seb looked down the underground river. It stretched far away from them. A crack ran through the ground above it, lighting up the long waterway. Bruke must have stood on a particularly weak spot along the crack. Were it not for the long line of light, they wouldn't have been able to see a thing.

"Where do you think it leads?" Bruke asked, voicing Seb's thoughts. "To the queen, maybe?"

Before Seb could answer him, the water splashed up by his feet. Not a large splash, but enough to command his attention. The movement went against the natural flow of the river.

Easy to dismiss the anomaly, Seb then heard a loud splash a distance away from them. Too far away to see. When he glanced at the others and saw the looks on their faces, he knew they'd heard it too.

As one, they all stood up and raised their weapons. A second later, another loud splash sounded out closer than the one that had preceded it. "Get ready," Seb said, his mouth drying, his pulse quickening. He lifted his rifle to his shoulder, closed one eye, and watched the water.

CHAPTER 63

The next loud splash introduced another pink creature. Larger than any they'd seen, it burst from the water like a giant seal. Seb's world slipped into slow motion as he watched the huge beast fly towards him. He pulled the trigger on his gun and sent a pulse of blasts into its face.

The first few green bolts hit the brute, but they did nothing. Then one landed square in the centre of its forehead. It sank in and blew a cloud of blue blood out of the back of its skull.

The force of the blast sent the beast's head backwards, its bum swinging around beneath it before it fell into the water, back first, with a loud splash.

Before the water had settled, another one burst from the river. Despite being the size of hippos, they leapt like salmon.

Bruke shot the next one. The same blue cloud of blood showed he'd killed the thing as it too fell back into the river with an almighty splash.

SA took down the third one. Unlike Bruke and Seb, she only needed one shot. A fourth, fifth, and sixth burst from the river and SA sent three more direct hits into them.

When the seventh and eighth creatures jumped out together, SA shot one and both Bruke and Seb went for the next one. They both missed, hitting its face with a barrage of blasts.

The beast continued to fly through the air at them, so Seb dropped his weapon, stepped forward, and met it with a heavy blow to its fat snout. A wet *clop* and he drove the creature back, its head flying away from them, spinning it over in a backwards somersault.

As it spun through the air, SA shot it in the forehead, turning the snapping brute limp. A loud splash met its collision with the river.

The blue of the creatures' oily blood ran through the water, but the pink bodies were nowhere to be seen.

"It must be deep," Seb said as he bent down to retrieve his gun. He aimed down at the river, waiting for more of them to come. More of them, or the grubs inside them.

CHAPTER 64

A few minutes had passed and no more of the pink creatures had jumped from the water. They might still have to deal with the grubs, but Seb lowered his gun all the same. He kept a hold of it should he need it, but at present, their way looked clear.

Seb turned to the other two, but before he spoke, he saw the shocked look on SA's face through her visor. "What is it?" he said.

When SA tapped her screen where the radiation monitor displayed the remaining time, Seb looked at his own and gasped. "What the ...? One hour left? What's that about? We had over *double* that a minute ago."

Suddenly the water looked very different. What Seb had assumed to be the effect of the creatures' blood now looked like something else entirely. Like a blue glow of radiation. It must have been why the trees were covered in tumours. If they used poisoned water to keep themselves alive, of course they'd look that way.

A look at SA and Seb saw her staring down at the rushing

water. She clearly thought the same as him, so he voiced it for both of them as he pointed down at the river. "The radiation on this planet's coming from there."

CHAPTER 65

"We've got to turn back," Bruke said as he backed away from the river, turned around, and reached up the wall to climb out of there.

But Seb didn't follow him. Instead, he said, "And turn our back on Sparks? We leave here now, and we've done *nothing* to help her. We might as well have got in the shuttle and blown up with Wilson and his family."

Bruke's face fell limp as he turned to look at Seb again. "You can't say that!"

"Don't get me wrong," Seb said, "I'm sad about what happened to Wilson and the others, of *course* I am. I just wanted to highlight the futility of coming into this forest if we're going to back out at the first sign of trouble."

"Radiation poisoning's more than trouble, Seb. If the radiation's coming from the water, which it seems like it is, and we get caught down here, what good are we to Sparks then?"

"About as much good as we are now. We've got to try. Besides," Seb said, "the time's adjusted. It's worked out how long we have down here. We still have an hour. That's enough time to give it a go. We just need to keep an eye on the clock."

For a second Bruke didn't reply. Then he pointed down the river. "Who's to say going down there's the right thing to do anyway?"

"Did you see those creatures?"

"Of *course* I did."

"They're much better suited for water than land. This must be their natural habitat."

"And?"

"They live down here. They *belong* down here. So if they're down here, maybe the parasites have found them and holed up with them. Maybe the queen is down here too."

"And if she's not?"

"Then we get back to the tank and think of another plan."

Bruke shook his head. "I don't like it."

"None of us *like* it, Bruke." The timer on Seb's screen had dropped to '55m' already. To look at it quickened his pulse. "We haven't got the time to discuss this. If you want to go back to the tank, you do that. I'll meet you there when I'm done."

Seb turned his back on Bruke and moved towards the river. The rock must have been wet, because when he stepped on it, his foot slipped. Although his gift served no purpose at that moment, panic sent his world into slow motion. Already falling, he had nothing to hold onto as he toppled towards the body of water. The water full of those huge creatures. The water potentially still crawling with the grubs inside of them and aglow with radiation.

A splash rang out as Seb broke the surface of the river. An adept swimmer, he didn't panic. At least, he didn't panic at first. Not until he started to sink.

CHAPTER 66

The first time Seb had tried to swim since he'd had his metal fists. They fell through the water like anchors, dragging him with them.

The stripe of light from the crack in the cave's ceiling faded the farther Seb sank into the river. The faster he fell, the more rapid his pulse beat until it thrummed through his skull. What about the parasites in the creatures they'd just killed? They would come out of the corpses at some point and find him pinned to the riverbed. Hopefully they couldn't swim.

When Seb looked down, he still couldn't see the bottom of the river. How would he get back up again when he reached the dark bed? Maybe it went straight to the planet's core.

And then he stopped. Almost like he'd reached the end of a bungee rope, something pulled beneath his armpits and halted his downward fall. But he didn't bounce back up like a bungee. Instead, he hung there, his rescuer's hands enough to halt his drop, but not enough to pull him back to the surface.

Seb turned and looked up into the bioluminescent gaze of

SA. Where she usually appeared composed, he saw the struggle in her pinched eyes. She couldn't drag him to the surface on her own.

When Seb kicked with her, it lifted them both a little closer to the shimmering crack of light above. Fortunately their suits were watertight. The press of the cold river might have pushed against him, but he remained dry and could still breathe.

They made slow progress and Seb's legs burned from the effort of the swim, but they beat gravity's pull as they edged closer to land. The shimmering strip of light above them grew brighter.

When they got close to breaking through, a hand reached down and grabbed the back of Seb's collar.

After Bruke had dragged Seb up onto the riverbank, Seb fell on his back, gasping and sweating from the effort of getting out of there. He watched Bruke hold a hand out to SA, who didn't need to take it as she climbed from the river on her own.

"Thank you," Seb said to SA, breathless from the effort of the swim. SA, on the other hand, looked like she'd waited beside the river for the entire time. Were she not wet, he wouldn't have been able to tell she'd exerted herself in any way.

A look from SA then down to Seb, Bruke said, "I suppose I have to go with you now, eh? I can't leave you to walk along the river in case you fall in again. I didn't realise you couldn't swim."

"I *can* swim," Seb said.

Bruke looked at the water. When he turned back to Seb, he raised his eyebrows.

Seb held his hands up. "It's the metal that made me sink. I didn't realise just how heavy they were until now."

"Come on," Bruke said, rolling his eyes at Seb as if he were lying. He tapped his visor where the timer was. "We don't have the time to stand around and chat."

CHAPTER 67

How hadn't he noticed it before then? In the commotion of sinking and being rescued, Seb had focused on his friends rather than his visor. Panic sat close to the surface since they'd landed on the damn planet, it now threatened to reach up and throttle him. "Uh, Bruke?" he said, the breath he'd only just got back running away from him again.

Bruke had walked away from them along a rocky ledge running alongside the toxic river. He stopped and turned to his friend.

"What time does your radiation reading say?"

A shift of Bruke's eyes from where he looked at his reading. He then looked back at Seb. "Forty-five minutes." He frowned. "Why?"

One final check and Seb's heart kicked. "Mine doesn't."

"What does yours say?" Bruke's familiar anxiety twisted through his face. "Please say it's longer."

"It says twenty-five. What about you, SA?"

SA pointed at Seb.

"Twenty-five too?"

She shrugged and held up her hands to show all her fingers.

"Thirty-five?"

She nodded.

"It must have been from going in the water," Bruke said, his voice lifting in pitch, his words coming out faster than before. "I reckon we should give it five more minutes at the most and head out of here back to that tank. We can't help Sparks if we're dead from radiation poisoning."

As much as Seb didn't want to agree with Bruke, he nodded. "You're right. Let's pick up the pace, then."

CHAPTER 68

They moved at a fast march and Seb stared into the river. "I wonder what happened to the parasites in those monsters we killed?" His voice rang through the damp tunnel.

"I don't know," Bruke said, "but if they want to stay away, I'm okay with that. I'd rather not ..." He stopped still.

The crack in the ceiling gave them enough light to guide their way, but Seb had to walk an extra few steps to realise exactly why his friend had halted. The stillness of the place forced him to speak in a whisper. "Good job we didn't turn back."

SA stepped up beside them, her sharp eyes scanning the vast open cave in front of them.

"You think this is it?" Bruke said, his voice also low.

They'd come to a massive underground lake. So large, Seb could only just see the other side of it despite the light coming in from above. He had to squint as he scanned the walls opposite them. When he saw it, he pointed across for Bruke and SA. "I'd say so."

Although Bruke kept his voice low, his clear panic drove it a bit louder when he said, "That's the queen?"

A grub the size of a cow huddled in a dark corner. Were it not waxy and white, they probably wouldn't have seen it. It looked pregnant like the last one, and pulsated with a writhing mass of fat little grubs inside it. A chill twisted through Seb. "I reckon so."

"But how will we cross the lake?"

Other than the sound of the river running into the larger body of water, Seb heard nothing else. So when the sharp static hiss of his radio went off before he could reply to Bruke, his stomach sank. The sound rang out like an explosion and echoed through the huge cave. Not anyone trying to get in contact with them, just a crackle from where Seb had left it on. The water might have been damn near glowing with radiation, but it clearly hadn't killed the radio when it had been submerged in it.

Seb's pulse trebled as the three of them stood at the edge of the lake in silence, frozen as they stared out at the grub on the other side.

"Maybe the grub is the only thing down here," Bruke said.

Before Seb could respond, the crash of breaking water erupted in front of them and a massive pink creature leapt into the air. The largest of the beasts he'd seen so far, he stumbled backwards as his world returned to slow motion.

CHAPTER 69

Just one of the creatures—even one of the largest ones Seb had seen—would have been easy to deal with. But straight after the first one burst from the water, several more of the fat pink beasts followed it. All of them leapt into the air as if catapulted towards them.

Seb, SA, and Bruke stood on a large outcropping of rock. Large enough to give them the room to step back a pace as the first of the beasts landed in front of them, shaking the ground it slammed down on.

A trumpeting roar that blew Seb back a step, and the frenzied thing rushed forward.

The outcropping had seemed large until they hit the wall behind them.

Several more of the beasts followed the first in bellyflopping onto the piece of rock with wet slaps. Each one ran a hard shock through the soles of Seb's feet.

Before the lead creature got any closer, they opened fire.

They looked good for it at first, taking down the large brute at the front with a shot to the head. Blue mist, it fell limp on the ground, but the others slid over the top of it as if it didn't exist, pushing it back behind them into the toxic lake.

A wall of red eyes, a wave of trumpeting fury, and the sloshing of their fat bellies sliding over the wet rock. They could overwhelm them at any second.

But Seb, SA, and Bruke took the next wave down. The gun shook in Seb's hands and he turned his focus to the ones behind the second wave. They burst from the water as if they would never end. More than the previous rush. Maybe too many.

Splash after splash of water broke the surface behind the front line of creatures. They took several down and twice the amount replaced them. They all slammed onto the hard rock, sending an earthquake through the ground.

Maybe Seb heard the crack of the rock splitting beneath his feet and maybe he didn't. However, if it sheared off, it would drag them into the water and they wouldn't come out again. He would sink like a rock and the other two didn't have the beating of the monsters in the lake. On land, they had the slimmest of chances. In the water, they had none. Not that they currently had any other options but to stand there and fight at that moment.

Seb's arms ached to hold his gun in place. It bucked and shook in his grip and turned the air green with laser fire. Many of his shots did little but hit the hard skin of the beasts in front of them. Every once in a while, he hit their weak spot and dropped them.

The *clunk* of Seb's gun jammed in his hands. When he looked down and saw the red light glowing from where it had overheated, his shoulders slumped.

A second later, Bruke's gun stopped too.

The pair looked at one another while SA continued to nail

the beasts. Every one of her shots scored a direct hit, but even with her accuracy she couldn't do it all on her own.

The splashing from the creatures continued to burst through the cave as they came forward in another rush. The thuds of the beasts continued to land on the rock. The crack of the rock beneath their feet continued to groan like thawing ice. Seb definitely hadn't imagined it.

Where Seb had seen fear in Bruke's wide brown eyes, they now narrowed. After hurling his gun at the closest beast, Bruke lost his head.

A roar to rival the one their enemy directed at them, Bruke turned into the creature Seb had seen when they'd fought the Crimson soldiers. He went supersonic, his arms moving in a chaotic swirl as he took the fight to their enemy.

As with his blaster fire, what Bruke lacked in accuracy, he made up for with frequency. Enough punches and kicks that some of them inevitably had to land. Several creatures fell beneath Bruke's heavy attack. SA took the others down. It forced the wave back.

While the other two fought their enemy, Seb looked down at the reading on his visor. It said '20m'.

They didn't have time to discuss anything now. Seb took SA's gun from her. At first, she held onto it and pulled it back. A dark glare, and for a moment, she looked like she could turn it on him.

"Trust me," Seb said. "Please?"

SA relaxed and handed the gun over.

The blasters were much more resilient than the automatic rifles, but when Seb looked down at the gauge on the top, it had a burnt orange glow to it. He looked at SA again. "How many shots do you think it has left?"

She held up one finger.

"Really?"

She nodded.

"Great!"

Bruke continued to drive the monsters back on his own. Those at the rear of the pack were forced to return to the lake.

Although Bruke had the advantage, when Seb looked across the large body of water, he saw the blue surface had turned pink with the sheer weight of beasts just beneath it. It didn't matter how well Bruke fought, they'd be overwhelmed soon enough.

One shot. Seb raised SA's blaster and pointed it across the cave. One shot to decide whether they lived or died. Whether Sparks lived or died.

A deep breath to settle his overworked heart and Seb closed one eye. It didn't matter how long he stared at the queen for, the shot wouldn't feel any easier. Despite SA having the best aim, he had to take the chance. Almost impossible odds, he couldn't put that on her shoulders.

Seb pulled the trigger, the gun kicking in his grip as he loosed a green bolt from it.

As the laser shot flew through the air, Seb tested the gun by squeezing its trigger again. SA had been correct. No shots left. He dropped the weapon on the ground. By the time it had cooled down, their fate would have been sealed.

Most of Seb's attention followed the green shot across the cave. However, he also noticed Bruke being forced back as the pink creatures started to gain an advantage. Not that the creatures mattered anymore. The shot would either be true or it wouldn't. That would decide everything.

And it did decide everything.

It missed.

CHAPTER 70

Seb's entire world crumbled around him as he watched splinters of rock burst away from where he'd shot. He'd missed by a good few metres. He nearly vomited. They were done for. Stuck in a cave, surrounded by hideous walrus-like creatures, and about to die in one of many ways. Drowning, mauling, radiation poisoning—what did it matter? They were screwed.

A look at SA and Seb saw her face limp behind her visor. He'd let everyone down, and as much as he would have liked to fast-forward to their end, he'd have to live every painful beat of it, his world still dragging along in slow motion.

A pop and crack ran through the rock platform. Seb jumped in anticipation of the ledge giving way. He looked down as if simply staring at the rock outcropping would somehow make everything better. Much more weight on it and they'd be in the toxic river. Minutes of radiation protection left and he'd see it out at the bottom of the water. If the beasts even allowed him that. Maybe they'd tear him to pieces before he hit the bottom. Or worse, they'd rip a leak in his suit and he would slowly drown, doing a strange handstand on the bed of the lake as his metal fists pinned him to the ground.

Bruke continued to fight against the creatures. He'd gained the advantage again, driving them back once more as the fat-bodied brutes slipped into the water. SA moved next to him. Were she able to open her suit, Seb had no doubt that she would have battled with her knives. But the radiation would get to her, so she used her fists, matching Bruke blow for blow.

When he heard another crack, Seb jumped again. But he hadn't felt it through his feet. Another look down at the rock. The darkness of their surroundings made it difficult to see where the cracks had formed. Although the two deep snaps told him he should be able to see them by now.

The third crack snapped like a whip. It definitely didn't come through the ground. He looked across the lake. Right there, next to the fat pulsating queen, sat the scorch mark from where he'd shot the blaster. Tendrils of cracks stretched away from the blackened point of impact. They grew as he watched them, lurching off from the centre.

Seb stepped back a pace while the other two fought the beasts. He kept his eyes on the rocks above the queen.

Before his back hit the wall, the ceiling above the queen collapsed. A heavy shower of large rocks landed on top of her.

The battle in front of him halted as the queen popped like a water balloon. Clear liquid burst away from her in a thick spray of pus. Thankfully Seb couldn't smell it. The sight alone snapped his stomach tense.

The pink beast closest to them looked at Bruke and SA. They both kept their fists raised, but they didn't attack it. It shook its head and its red eyes suddenly turned yellow. It stared in curiosity at the two before it looked past them at Seb.

The creature's cheeks then bulged and it vomited in front of them. A thick grub fell from its mouth and landed on the rock outcropping. Dead. Limp.

When the pink beast looked up again, all of its rage had left it. Passive inquiry stared at them now rather than fury and the desire to destroy.

A ripple effect ran away from the first creature, the other pink beasts all vomiting at different times. Dead and limp grubs landed on the ground and fell into the water. The ones Seb could see all looked the same. They glistened with the bile of the pink creatures.

One by one, the pink beasts looked over at Seb and the others with yellow serenity.

Seb felt both SA and Bruke look at him as he watched the creatures. A glance at one and then the other before he shrugged. "I'm guessing we got the queen, then?"

Before either answered him, Seb looked down at the reading on his screen. When he saw the timer, he gasped, the sound of it echoing through his helmet. "We have ten minutes to get out of here."

Although Seb and the others tried to step forward, the creatures moved across to block their way. The calm and inquisitive stares now looked more resolute and assertive. They weren't moving. Seb and the other two had killed many of their kin. They might have been naturally passive, but the looks on their faces suggested they wanted retribution.

CHAPTER 71

The sound of hundreds of the pink beasts broke the water's surface one after the other. "All this," Seb said as he remained where he stood, pinned in by the creatures, "and now they're going to tear us apart. Don't they see we've freed so many of them?"

Neither SA nor Bruke had time to react to his words before the creatures parted in front of them. Several of the large brutes floated in the water right by the stone ledge.

"What are they doing?" Bruke said.

Seb could only shake his head as he looked at the bobbing beasts. They were lined up as ships would in a dock. "I don't know. They don't look like they want to attack us."

When Seb tried to walk away from the lake in the direction of the path alongside the river, one of the pink-skinned brutes blocked his way.

"But they don't want to let us go either," Bruke said.

It took for SA to walk forward for Seb to see their intention. As she headed in the direction of the creatures in the water, the ones on land gave her an opening to pass through.

Both Seb and Bruke watched her step onto the back of

one of them. It moved forward with her and another one replaced it next to the stone platform.

"They want us to ride on them?" Bruke said.

"It would seem so."

"You think we should?"

"SA does, and that's good enough for me." Seb walked to the lakeside and stepped onto the back of another one of the creatures. It shifted forwards a few metres so another could come in behind for Bruke.

The creatures had long enough necks for them to raise their heads from the water. SA gripped around it, so Seb and Bruke copied her.

The second Bruke—as the last one to do it—held on, the creatures took off up the river.

Because of the tight river and their large bodies, the creatures moved in single file back the way the three friends had come from. They moved so fast, the sides of Seb's containment suit flapped in his ears and he had to grip on hard. If he lost his concentration, he'd be at the bottom of the river in seconds, and his radiation protection would run out.

The journey would have taken most of their ten minutes had they done it on foot. When they jumped off the creatures at the end of the river, Seb looked at his visor. He had eight minutes left.

Before they could leave, each creature dropped their head and nuzzled their passenger.

"I think they're thanking us," Bruke said with a laugh as his creature nearly knocked him over.

Seb couldn't help but smile when he tickled his one beneath the chin.

As one, the three beasts trumpeted their thanks at Seb and the others before they disappeared beneath the water and vanished back down towards the underground lake.

Clearly giddy from the experience, Bruke said, "That was amazing."

But they didn't have time for that. They could discuss it later. Seven minutes left before Seb's suit became ineffective. "Come on," he said. "Let's get out of here."

CHAPTER 72

The second Seb got clear of the hole, his radiation reading changed. "It's doubled my time," he said. "What about you two?"

"I have forty minutes now," Bruke said.

"I only have fifteen," Seb replied. "What about you, SA?"

SA held both hands up to show ten, closed her hands and opened them again.

"Twenty minutes?" Seb said.

She nodded.

He had been in the water longer than her. "Well, even fifteen should be enough. Come on, let's get out of here."

The blue and red bracken and tumour trees took on a different meaning now Seb had seen what fed them. No doubt poison ran through the forest like it did the river beneath it. It seemed okay for the pink creatures, but the thing that sustained a lot of the life here appeared to also poison it. He shuddered to think of Moses. An apt comparison.

"I feel bad for the ones we killed," Bruke said as they moved through the forest at a fast march.

Seb sighed. "Me too." When he looked at SA, she didn't

give much away. "But we had to. And you know what? If we hadn't killed them, we wouldn't have got to the queen down in the lake."

"That's true," Bruke said.

"And think of all the ones we just saved by taking down the queen," Seb added.

Although SA had led for most of their journey through the woods, Seb overtook her towards the edge and stepped out into the barren desert first.

A second later, SA and Bruke joined him.

The three of them stood there for a second and stared out at the red wasteland. Seb shrugged. "Where the hell's the tank?"

CHAPTER 73

Eight minutes wouldn't get them very far in the expansive desert. It would take them hours to walk back to the hangar, and the Shadow Order's shuttle now existed as a twisted wreck somewhere in Carstic's wilderness.

"That's it, then," Seb said, throwing his hands up in the air before he sat down on the hard ground. "That's the end of that. After everything we've been through, and we now have no way of getting back to the hangar."

"What do you think's happened?" Bruke said as he paced up and down, shaking his head.

"She's woken up, hasn't she."

"And left us?"

"I can't imagine she knew what else to do. She probably couldn't remember anything from when she was under."

"But we tied her up," Bruke said.

Seb let out a laugh. It died as quickly as his hope had. "Have you not met Sparks? I'd imagine she's back at the hangar right now, looking for a ship to fly herself off this cursed planet."

Bruke's shoulders slumped and he turned his head to the side. "You think?"

"She wouldn't have known we were still in the forest. What else could she do?"

Bruke sighed and sat down next to Seb. A second later, SA did the same. Seb and the other two stared across the arid wasteland, the bright sun slightly dulled because of the yellow tint to his visor. He shook his head. "What a way to go."

CHAPTER 74

Seb watched another minute of his radiation timer tick away. Four minutes left. He sighed again. If he had to go out like this, he at least wanted SA to know how he felt about her.

Just as he turned to her, the loud roar of a vehicle came at them from across the desert. As one, all three of them looked up to see the tank tearing towards them. The vehicle shook as it travelled over the hard and bumpy ground.

The tank hurtled towards them at what looked like full throttle before the vehicle turned sideways, skidding to a halt. A second later, the door at the back opened.

Bruke jumped to his feet and ran into the vehicle first. SA looked at Seb like she knew he'd wanted to say something.

Seb stood up, held his hand down to her and then showed her the way with a sweeping arm gesture. "Ladies first." He'd tell her what he wanted to another time.

Just before Seb followed SA into the back of the tank, he looked at the forest one last time. After shaking his head, he smiled to himself and walked into the vehicle, his legs burning with exhaustion, his entire body made of lead.

The door closed behind them as Sparks spun around in the driver's seat and smiled. "Why did you tie me up?"

"You don't know?" Bruke said.

The familiar purple glow lit up Sparks' eyes and she laughed. "I'm guessing it has something to do with that thing I threw up?" She pointed at the ground.

Seb had nearly stepped on it. A grub—small like the ones that crawled from the people in the mines—lay dead on the floor of the tank.

"Now strap in," Sparks said. "I'm going to get us out of here."

It felt great to sit down. It didn't matter how hard the bench, Seb sank onto it and leaned back against the wall of the vehicle. The grubs had been taken down and his friend had returned. Everything else would be just fine.

CHAPTER 75

The front window of the tank showed Seb they were closing down on the hangar. Sparks could fly any of the ships to get them out of there. He leaned forward and picked up the dead grub she'd vomited out. It still glistened with bile.

When Seb sat back, he saw both SA and Bruke staring at him. "What are you doing?" Bruke said.

"Wilson said he thought the grubs were dropped on this planet on purpose. I'm inclined to believe him. I want to take this in case it gives me any clues."

"Do you really believe that?" Bruke said.

"Ruthane's worth a lot of money. Wilson said that where there are credits, there's often corruption. I think he's right. I don't think his ship going down was an accident. And if it wasn't, I owe it to him and his family to find out the truth. After all, they gave us the information that saved Sparks."

A shake of his head and Bruke sat back in his seat. "I'm too tired to think about it."

"Me too," Seb replied. "But I'm not too tired to forget

about it." He held the grub up. "If I take this for now, I can look into it when I get the time."

The hangar doors opened up as they got close to it, and Seb looked down at the reading on his screen. Just three minutes left. "You think we can get out of here soon, Sparks?" he said. "My radiation suit won't last much longer."

"Don't worry," Sparks called back at him. "I'll have us off this planet in sixty seconds. Get ready to change vehicles."

Seb smiled at his friend. "Although you're a little rat, I've missed you. I'm glad you're all right."

Sparks threw the hand gesture he'd seen from her in the past. One of these days he'd have to ask her exactly what the insult meant.

END OF BOOK FOUR.

∽

Thank you for reading Eradication - Book Four of The Shadow Order.

∽

Want more of the Shadow Order? Reyes becomes an important member of the Shadow Order from book five onwards. Get to know her in 120-Seconds: A Shadow Order Story - available at www.michaelrobertson.co.uk

Support the Author

Dear reader, as an independent author I don't have the resources of a huge publisher. If you like my work and would like to see more from me in the future, there are two things you can do to help: leaving a review, and a word-of-mouth referral.

Releasing a book takes many hours and hundreds of dollars. I love to write, and would love to continue to do so. All I ask is that you leave a review on the store you bought the book from. It shows other readers that you've enjoyed the book and will encourage them to give it a try too. The review can be just one sentence, or as long as you like.

∼

IF YOU'D LIKE TO BE NOTIFIED OF SPECIAL OFFERS, NEWS, AND new releases, you can sign up to my spam-free mailing list at www.michaelrobertson.co.uk

ABOUT THE AUTHOR

Like most children born in the seventies, Michael grew up with Star Wars in his life. An obsessive watcher of the films, and an avid reader from an early age, he found himself taken over with stories whenever he let his mind wander.

Those stories had to come out.

He hopes you enjoy reading his books as much as he does writing them.

Michael loves to travel when he can. He has a young family, who are his world, and when he's not reading, he enjoys walking so he can dream up more stories.

Contact

www.michaelrobertson.co.uk
subscribers@michaelrobertson.co.uk

ALSO BY MICHAEL ROBERTSON

The Shadow Order
The First Mission - Book Two of The Shadow Order
The Crimson War - Book Three of The Shadow Order
Eradication - Book Four of The Shadow Order
120-Seconds: A Shadow Order Story

∼

The Alpha Plague: A Post-Apocalyptic Action Thriller
The Alpha Plague 2
The Alpha Plague 3
The Alpha Plague 4
The Alpha Plague 5
The Alpha Plague 6
The Alpha Plague 7
The Alpha Plague 8

∼

Crash - A Dark Post-Apocalyptic Tale
Crash II: Highrise Hell
Crash III: There's No Place Like Home
Crash IV: Run Free
Crash V: The Final Showdown

New Reality: Truth

New Reality 2: Justice

New Reality 3: Fear

OTHER AUTHORS UNDER THE SHIELD
OF PHALANX PRESS

Sixth Cycle

Nuclear war has destroyed human civilization.

Captain Jake Phillips wakes into a dangerous new world, where he finds the remaining fragments of the population living in a series of strongholds, connected across the country. Uneasy alliances have maintained their safety, but things are about to change. -- Discovery **leads to danger.** -- Skye Reed, a tracker from the Omega stronghold, uncovers a threat that could spell the end for their fragile society. With friends and enemies revealing truths about the past, she will need to decide who to trust. -- Sixth **Cycle** is a gritty post-apocalyptic story of survival and adventure.

Darren Wearmouth ~ Carl Sinclair

~

DEAD ISLAND: Operation Zulu

Ten years after the world was nearly brought to its knees by a zombie Armageddon, there is a race for the antidote! On a remote Caribbean island, surrounded by a horde of hungry living dead, a team of American and Australian commandos must rescue the Antidotes' scientist. Filled with zombies, guns, Russian bad guys, shady government types, serial killers and elevator muzak. Dead Island is an action packed blood soaked horror adventure.

Allen Gamboa

Invasion Of The Dead Series

This is the first book in a series of nine, about an ordinary bunch of friends, and their plight to survive an apocalypse in Australia. -- Deep beneath defense headquarters in the Australian Capital Territory, the last ranking Army chief and a brilliant scientist struggle with answers to the collapse of the world, and the aftermath of an unprecedented virus. Is it a natural mutation, or does the infection contain -- more sinister roots? -- One hundred and fifty miles away, five friends returning from a month-long camping trip slowly discover that death has swept through the country. What greets them in a gradual revelation is an enemy beyond compare. -- Armed with dwindling ammunition, the friends must overcome their disagreements, utilize their individual skills, and face unimaginable horrors as they battle to reach their hometown...

Owen Ballie

Whiskey Tango Foxtrot

Alone in a foreign land. The radio goes quiet while on convoy in Afghanistan, a lost patrol alone in the desert. With his unit and his home base destroyed, Staff Sergeant Brad Thompson suddenly finds himself isolated and in command of a small group of men trying to survive in the Afghan wasteland. **Every turn leads to danger**

The local population has been afflicted with an illness that turns them into rabid animals. They pursue him and his men at every corner and stop. Struggling to hold his team together and unite survivors, he must fight and evade his way to safety. **A fast paced zombie war story like no other.**

W.J. Lundy

∼

Zombie Rush

New to the Hot Springs PD Lisa Reynolds was not all that welcomed by her coworkers especially those who were passed over for the position. It didn't matter, her thirty days probation ended on the same day of the Z-poc's arrival. Overnight the world goes from bad to worse as thousands die in the initial onslaught. National Guard and regular military unit deployed the day before to the north leaves the city in mayhem. All directions lead to death until one unlikely candidate steps forward with a plan. A plan that became an avalanche raging down the mountain culminating in the salvation or destruction of them all.

Joseph Hansen

∼

The Gathering Horde

The most ambitious terrorist plot ever undertaken is about to be put into motion, releasing an unstoppable force against humanity. Ordinary people – A group of students celebrating the end of the semester, suburban and rural families – are about to themselves in the center of something that threatens the survival of the human species. As they battle the dead – and the living – it's going to take every bit of skill, knowledge and luck for them to survive in Zed's World.

Rich Baker

Printed in Great Britain
by Amazon